INVESTMENTS

M. F. A. Dillon

Second Edition

February 7, 2012

For my father, James Dillon,

who made wise investments

of time and energy

Table of Contents

	Page
The Consulate	7
The Lion of Córdoba	13
The Woods	17
Year Abroad	23
High Society	33
Transcendence	45
The Desert	59
The Christmas Orphan	67
A Verona Interlude	73
Instinct	77
La Gourmande	85
Donnybrook	99
Spanish Lessons	117
Win-Lose Games	125
The Diablo Mystery	135
The Reunion	145

	Page
The Tragedy of Cyber Contra	153
The Colombian Eight Escudos Piece	159
The Baltic Memorandum	167
The Case of the Disappearing Library	177
The Escalon Inscriptions	185
Providence	193
A Fortune	199

The Consulate

      The antechamber to the office of the consul of Lustre was dominated at one end by a young woman seated at an extensive desk. Ensconced behind a computer, she was occupied with working on an article lauding the travel pleasures of her country. From time to time she interrupted her literary travails to take a telephone call and occasionally tiptoed into the consul's office to conduct some business of importance.

      Scattered about the antechamber, an oblong room carpeted by a light blue Persian rug bordered with an intricate crimson design, were end tables filled with travel magazines and pastel blue or yellow armchairs. Some of these armchairs boasted occupants, but these were widely separated as if each wanted a space in which to think his own thoughts.

      Julian Friedlander was one of the uncommunicative occupants of the consul's antechamber that morning. He fished a *Times* out of his briefcase and made a pretense of reading. Soon, however, the news of wars and disasters, the editorialized political reportage and the tired sameness of it all drove him back on his own thoughts. He folded the paper and looked at his watch. It was 11:15 a.m., the time designated for his appointment, and there were two other applicants for residency visas ahead of him, a woman around age 35 and an elderly gentleman. Julian could tell they were applicants because they had a certain anxious look about them. They, too, had heard that not all residency visa applications were approved, and they wondered if they would be one of the lucky ones.

Julian did not dwell long on reviewing the chances of the other applicants. It was his own history that preoccupied his thoughts. He would be telling the consul his story shortly so he put away his newspaper and went over again what he would say.

He was thirty – not old, not young. He had started out in life living in the land of Gloom and had considered himself to be a reasonably happy fellow. He had two reasonably happy parents and a younger sister named Flossie who used to look at him with stars in her eyes. Now he never saw her. She had married and moved away, and they were in touch only sporadically.

When Julian was growing up, he had thought that Gloom was a normal place. At least he had never been anywhere else. He had an uncle who lived in Lustre and who came for visits once or twice a year. His uncle had urged Julian to learn the language of Lustre, but his parents gave him no encouragement in this idea as they did not want him to leave them. Consequently, he had never studied Lustrian nor taken seriously the idea of moving to that country. Eventually he had finished his schooling and had settled down to work as a lawyer. He had built up a successful practice and had looked forward to a reasonably happy life.

But things had turned out differently. His uncle died, and somehow the happiness that Julian had previously experienced died with him. He began to feel the full impact of living in Gloom.

The door to the consul's office opened and a young man came out carrying some papers and beaming broadly. He smiled at the receptionist and exchanged some pleasantries with her. Then he stuffed the papers he was carrying into his attaché case and walked out. A moment later the consul appeared and asked the young woman to come into his office.

The young lady reminded Julian of Augusta. He had met Augusta Hunt a couple of years previously. She had a polished social personality, was wealthy, and gave Julian access to an exclusive country club where he met a number of potential clients, but she never looked at him with stars in her eyes. Augusta did not know anyone in Lustre and seemed content to be reasonably happy in Gloom.

Wondering how he could best present his case to the consul, Julian came to the conclusion that he had no case. He just had a vague desire to go to Lustre. He knew visas were not granted automatically. One had to offer something special.

Looking out the window, Julian noted how bleak the landscape was. A wintry wind buffeted the skeletons of trees. A branch rattled on the windowpane. Julian struggled to keep the desolation of the winter scene from finding a mirror in his psyche.

The consul's door opened, and the young woman reappeared. She looked grim and closed her eyes briefly, as if wishing to keep her sorrow to herself. She left quickly, her lips buttoned up.

The old man was next. Julian fidgeted. Lustre had seemed so remote when he was a child. Gloom was represented as normal, but now he saw it as a relatively cheerless place in which to live. He had not realized when he was growing up how fragile his happiness was. In

Gloom obscurity was paramount, and people maintained a semblance of civilized behavior amid obfuscations of every type. Truth was not held in high esteem. When Julian reflected on it, he came to the conclusion that any happiness found in Gloom was due to some clarity coming from Lustre, a land running on entirely different premises. In Lustre the sun shone as a matter of course, and people reflected that light with sunny dispositions. Gloom, in contrast, was usually cloudy although the sun broke through the haze occasionally around someone who was in some way connected to Lustre. Julian had sought out friends who had a little of this light about them, and so he felt reasonably happy.

The old man came out of the consul's office. He paused and looked soberly at Julian. "Good luck" was all he said before disappearing into the melancholy landscape outside.

The consul beckoned, and Julian stepped into his office. It was spacious and airy and decorated along the same lines as the antechamber. Next to the consul's desk stood a Lustrian flag. Some shelves along the walls were filled with books indicating classical tastes. A photograph of the consul's family sat atop a bookcase. A portrait of Queen Philippa of Lustre hung on one wall. Julian had heard that she ruled more by benevolent example than by fiat. He did not understand this; he thought it was one of the mysteries of Lustre.

"And what can I do for you?" the consul asked. He was a middle-aged man with a cheery demeanor. Julian decided to tell him everything – how he was interested in Lustre, how he had been studying the language lately on his own, and how his uncle who lived in Lustre had died, and he was no longer so happy living in Gloom.

"What was your uncle's name?" the consul asked.

"Austin MacKenzie."

"Austin MacKenzie? Why, I knew him. He was one of the queen's councillors and a personal friend of mine. He wrote popular history books."

"Really!" exclaimed Julian. "He never mentioned anything about what he did. He just talked about what interested us."

"The apple doesn't fall far from the tree," observed the consul. "Since Austin was your uncle, I will be happy to issue you a visa."

Julian hesitated.

The Lion of Córdoba

Oscar sat ensconced in his afternoon Spanish class at Washington Irving High School in mid-Manhattan and thought about the world. He was a young man small in stature and somewhat intense under his composure. His hair rose in a high permanent wave above his forehead, and he sported a jacket emblazoned with the words "*Leones de Córdoba.*"

Oscar felt relaxed in Spanish class. Señora Brown rarely called on him, and when she did, he could easily engage her in conversation. Spanish was easy for him. Indeed, it was his first language. This did not mean that he wa not in danger of flunking Spanish as he was in danger of flunking all his subjects. It was the grammar. Spanish grammar was not spoken at home. Oscar was first introduced to it in Señora Brown's class, and it seemed difficult and unnecessary. After all, he could speak the language, and that was all that mattered.

Señora Brown was calling his name. She was a middle-aged woman wrapped in conventionality. Señora Brown ran a tight ship, and few dared to defy her authority though many dared to fail her course, all her efforts to the contrary. She wanted to quiz him on the subjunctive. Fill in the blanks. "*Pasaremos tiempo en Madrid para que tú ...*" Oscar faltered, and Señora Brown went on the query someone else.

Oscar returned to his ruminations. His parents had come to the United States from Central America almost twenty years ago. They worked in a fast food restaurant, his father as a cashier and his mother as a chef. His older sister María Elena left school when she was seventeen and was working in a dry cleaning establishment. With three incomes the family was able to rent a nice apartment and afford a few of the amenities. Oscar thought it was a good life and had decided to leave school and find a job as a cashier like his father when he turned seventeen.

It was Senora Brown again. Now she was requesting his input on the subjunctive for irregular verbs. "*Dar, dé, estar, esté, haber, haya, ir, vaya, saber, sepa, ser, sea.*" Subjunctive, subjunctive. They never spoke in the subjunctive at home. Oscar longed for the bell.

Eventually the bell rang, and Oscar moved in a vector toward his World History class. There was a lot of jostling in the corridor, and Oscar had to be particularly careful to avoid an occasional elbow in his ribs or fist in his face. "Oh, sorry!" they all said. It occurred to Oscar one day that he was getting more than his share of pokes and jabs on account of his diminuitive stature. That was when he decided to get a permanent wave. He had found a compliant barber who engineered an additional two or three inches of height for him. This seemed to help him negotiate the corridors of Washington Irving High School with fewer collisions.

Oscar arrived in Mr. Stanhope's World History class with only moments to spare. Nonchalantly he took his usual seat in the last row. Mr. Stanhope was a dapper young fellow with a freshly minted college degree who had the theory that anecdotal history was at least as interesting as historical change. Oscar enjoyed his class because Mr. Stanhope gave insights into historical personages. When they covered the fall of the Roman Republic, for instance, Mr. Stanhope had them read Marc Antony's funeral oration for Julius Caesar, or at least Shakespeare's version of it. Oscar found it all very interesting, but this did not have a noticeable impact on his grades.

Today Mr. Stanhope was addressing the rabble on the topic of Christian missionary activity in the Dark Ages. Oscar was nodding a bit when suddenly he heard his name. He jerked awake, surprised that Mr. Stanhope was calling on him. But Mr. Stanhope was not calling on him; he was talking about St. Oscar. Oscar sat up as straight as his permanent wave and pricked up his ears.

Mr. Stanhope was saying that St. Oscar joined a Benedictine monastery near Amiens in the ninth century and then, still in his twenties, traveled to Denmark and Sweden to convert the pagans to Christianity. His remarkable success in this endeavor attracted the attention of the pope, and soon Oscar was named the first bishop of Hamburg and later the archbishop of Bremen and Hamburg. In time he became known as the Apostle of the North.

Oscar jumped a little in his seat. His patron saint was the Apostle of the North? That was mind-blowing. Oscar was blown away by the concept.

The bell rang, and school was out. Oscar forwent his usual extracurricular activity of hanging out in front of the school with his friends and watching the girls. He wanted to be alone in order to think. For the rest of the afternoon he cogitated on his patron saint and his achievements. In the end he drew up some resolutions. He wanted to have an adventurous life like St. Oscar and so he decided to study Latin and to excel in school. He thought education was the key to success and adventure in the modern era.

The next day Oscar's hair still stood two or three inches above his forehead, and he still wore a jacket inscribed *"Leones de Córdoba."* He still went to Washington Irving High School in mid-Manhattan, and he was still in Señora Brown's Spanish class and Mr. Stanhope's World History class, but on the inside Oscar was a different person, and no one had the least idea why.

The Woods

Crispin was in a dark place. He looked around but could hardly see anything. He had come to a dark place in the woods where very little light penetrated. He listened for voices to find out if anyone was nearby. There was not a single sound. Perhaps people were close by but were sleeping. He shouted, but there was no response. He waited for several hours and then shouted again, but nothing had changed. The darkness continued, and so did the silence. Crispin was nonplussed. This had never happened before. There had always been people nearby; there had always been enough light to maneuver by. Crispin thought about how he had come to this place in the woods.

He had not grown up in the woods. He had grown up in Mendelein, a small town in the rural heartland where his parents were well-respected and relatively prosperous. He had known nothing of the woods except that it existed. It was far away from Mendelein, and nobody in town seemed interested in it.

Then Crispin went away to college. He chose Westerleigh University, a well-known institution about a hundred miles distant from Mendelein, because it had a country club campus and the woman who interviewed him smiled and said all the right things. This was paradise, Crispin thought, and so he had worked his way through the complicated application process with his heart set on going to Westerleigh University and Westerleigh University alone.

Thus it was with a sense of triumph that Crispin received the letter telling him that he had been admitted. He felt he would not only be going to a prestigious university, but also to one where the courses would not be too strenuous and where thee was a sense of community.

It was only after orientation was over and classes had begun that Crispin met Adrian. He remembered it later quite well. Adrian's first comment had been "Cri-i-i-spin? Where did you get a name like that?"

Crispin was used to such reactions, and so he replied nonchalantly, "My mother heard it once in a Shakespeare play. She liked the sound of it, and so she wished it on me." Then he added, "And where did you get the name Adrian?"

"When I was on the way, my mother was checking out a baby book for possible names and came across it. She thought it sounded cute, and so she popped it on me. Later I looked it up and found out that several Roman emperors and some saints and popes have this name."

"So you're in good company," said Crispin.

"I guess so. Not to change the subject, but have you been to the woods yet? I was there the other day and am dying to go back. Want to go with me?"

This was the first Crispin had heard of the woods. Of course, he had known they existed, but here at Westerleigh? That was news to him. It turned out that the woods were fairly close to campus, and people often went walking there. Adrian told Crispin about the good times to be had in the woods. Crispin began to be interested, albeit he had an idea that the people who lived in Mendelein would have been surprised.

After a month or two it seemed that almost everyone had been to the woods except himself, and he did not want to be different. He decided to find out what was so intriguing. And so one Sunday morning, having nothing else to do, Crispin took a walk in the woods.

The woods were cool and pleasant. He had lots of company. He saw Adrian and some other friends there, and several parties were in progress. Crispin decided to visit the woods more often. When in Rome, do as the Romans, he thought.

This he did, only staying away when he was on vacation at home in Mendelein. There everyone was living as before, and Crispin slipped into his old ways.

When he returned to Westerleigh, however, he headed for the woods at the first opportunity. He began to explore pleasures other than socializing. At first he tried to get Adrian to go with him, but the latter demurred.

"My grandma is worried about my being in the woods. I think I had better not go any farther or she'll be bugging me about it. Sorry!"

Crispin decided to go exploring by himself. He was not concerned about going deeper into the woods although soon he found himself in a darker area where there were not so many people. He had become so intrigued by exploring what the woods had to offer that he decided to ignore the negatives in favor of experiencing new and more exotic pleasures.

Then one day he got lost. He had gone so far that he did not know his way back anymore. He had called out for help, and in a few minutes had attracted the attention of some nearby revelers who helped him find his way back to Westerleigh. Crispin was a bit shaken by this experience but a few days later decided to venture into the woods again.

Again he went too far and lost his way. Again he shouted for help, and help had arrived. This pattern had repeated itself several times, and so Crispin was not worried about going deeper into the woods.

This time, however, was different. This time no one responded to his shouts. This time he truly was lost. There were no human beings around. There were not even any animals. Crispin could hear nothing, and he could see hardly anything, the darkness was so great.

Crispin began to regret coming into the woods. He began to regret ever having heard of the woods. He wished he had never seen the woods. He knew there were people at Westerleigh who had nothing to do with the woods. They were the strong ones. They were the wise ones. He had drifted away from them. He thought if he ever got out of the woods, he would go back to being their friend. Actually, he began to wish he had never come to Westerleigh. It was too close to the woods. Crispin knew there were other universities that were not so close to the woods. He should have been more interested in them.

Crispin was beginning to sweat. He tried shouting again, but it was no use. There was no one anywhere in the vicinity.

"O God!" he exclaimed. "O dear God, what is going to happen to me?"

Just then he saw something white shimmering up ahead of him between the trees. It was moving in his direction. Crispin tried to shout, but he was so frightened that nothing emerged from his throat. "O dear God!" he thought to himself.

"Hello? Anyone here?" a voice from the shimmering white entity inquired.

Crispin found his voice. "It's me! I'm here!" he called out.

The white figure paused and then surged forward. "Rest easy, young man. I find lost humans regularly. Now that you have accessed the magic, I'll have you home in no time. Just hold on to my cloak." A kindly face ringed in curls beamed down at him, and Crispin was inclined to trust him. He grasped the stranger's cloak.

Suddenly they were back at Westerleigh. Crispin was blown away by the word "magic" and its aftermath.

The stranger looked at him gravely and said, "I hope you will remember your good resolutions and keep to them, young man. Bye." With these words he vanished, and Crispin shuffled back to college life, sure that he did not want to enter the woods again and not so sure that Westerleigh was paradise.

Year Abroad

On a certain Friday afternoon, in the season the French call St. Martin's summer, a halcyon blue sky complicated by a few fleecy white clouds hung over the Latin Quarter in Paris. Here and there students with earnest expressions on their faces hurried through cavernous streets to their classes at the Sorbonne. Blane Winterton wore this same earnest expression as he emerged from the Metro and, absorbed in recollecting a passage from Lamartine, walked along the Boulevard Saint-Michel toward the university. He looked neither to the left nor the right at the students chatting at tables scattered under the lime trees of the Place de la Sorbonne. Stepping along crisply, he entered the scholars' sanctum with a few minutes to spare before class was to begin. His concentration broken by the change of milieu, he decided to check his e-mail. A message from Avery popped up on the screen.

"Loved your last note. I'm kinda glad you miss me. I miss you too.

"My English prof wants a ten-page paper on the works of a nineteenth century writer. I'll probably do Jane

Austen. I've already read a coupla her novels so I'll read one more, and that should be enough. Whatcha think?

"Barney says hi. He says you're gonna come back speaking French instead of English.

"Take care. Luv ya."

Blane smiled. Avery was always informal even though she was an English major.

Blane remembered the call from his mother the night before. His mother had no time for Avery. She had met her twice and had formed an opinion. "She doesn't emote," she said. "She has a pleasant social personality, but the inner woman is out to lunch." Blane was into a kissing relationship with Avery by this time so he continued to date her but did not bring her home anymore. Nonetheless, his mother sensed her ongoing presence in his life and worried that he was heading into an unhappy marriage. She tried to interest him in other girls. On the telephone she had told me that Barbara McMahon, a girl he had graduated with from Lyndonville High, was taking courses at the Sorbonne. He had heard that her father had been appointed ambassador to France, but he had not heard anything further. His mother urged him to look Barbara up.

Actually, Blane had had a crush on Barbara all senior year of high school. She did not know about this. He had admired her from afar, attending three performances of "My Fair Lady" just to see her play the role of Eliza Doolittle, but he considered her a star out of his orbit and so had made no effort to introduce himself.

If she had been a star in high school, she was even more brilliantly placed now that her father was the ambassador to France. Blane felt he could never call her up at the embassy. She would not remember him and she might even laugh that he could be so naïve as to imagine that she would be interested in him. No, Blane had no intention of doing anything to precipitate a meeting with Barbara.

It was a Friday night, and he thought he might go to a production of "Le Bourgeois Gentilhomme" that was on the boards at a theatre in Saint-Germain-des-Prés. His friends were going to see an American movie, but Blane thought he would pass on that and have a French experience instead.

After a leisurely dinner in a café on the Boulevard Saint-Michel, he walked the distance to the theatre, invested in a ticket, and claimed a seat in the last row. Slowly the theatre filled up with a student crowd interspersed with some older couples. Blane opened his program and received the shock of his life. There in letters as plain as day it said that Barbara McMahon was playing the role of Dorimène. Blane stared at the program. It could not be someone else; it had to be she. How many Barbara McMahons could be doing theatre in Paris? It was the same. He had to hand it to her for starring in a French play. She must have a good accent. He remembered that she had visited some French cousins every summer. Blane settled back in his seat, wondering if she were as magical as ever.

Blane enjoyed every minute of what turned out to be a memorable production. He laughed heartily at M. Jourdain's antics as he fought to overcome his middle class upbringing in order to impress a daughter of the nobility. Barbara performed brilliantly. Her blonde hair floated over a perfect face and form. Her voice was clarion and persuasive, making her adorable to both the men on the stage and those in the audience. Blane was suffused with feelings he could not define.

That was why, when the performance ended, he could not bring himself to leave the theatre. When Barbara reappeared in street clothes, Blane was mesmerized. She lingered for a few moments talking to a fellow actor, then headed down the aisle on her way out of the theatre. He rose without thinking from his seat, and she glanced at him.

"Oh, hello!" she said hesitantly, slowing her step. "Don't I know you from somewhere?"

"Yes," replied Blane. "From Lyndonville High. We graduated in the same class."

"Oh!" She came to a halt, and a look of recognition flit over her lovely features. She smiled at him. "I remember you. You were in my English class in senior year. You always knew the answers to the most complicated questions."

"Yes," said Blane modestly. "My mother liked to discuss my English assignments with me."

"So your mother got an A!" she quipped.

"Yes," said Blane. "When I got to college, I was hard put to keep up the good work."

"I'm sure you held your own. Say, what are you doing here in Paris?"

"Going to the theatre."

"I don't believe you came to Paris just for a theatre weekend."

"Well, no. Actually I'm over at the Sorbonne, trying to become civilized."

"Oh, how nice! I'm going to the Sorbonne now too," said Barbara.

"I know," said Blane. She looked surprised. "I heard it from the grapevine, but the place is so large, I didn't think we would ever meet."

She made a motion to leave, and he fell into step alongside her, still talking and enjoying the moment. In this fashion they gained the street and made their way in pleasant conversation toward the Metro. They became so engrossed in humorous recollection of life at Lyndonville High that Blane followed her onto the subway platform almost without realizing it. When the train pulled in a few minutes later, it just seemed natural to get on with her in order not to interrupt the conversation. A little while later they were standing at the embassy gate, and he found himself asking her when they could see each other again. It turned out that she was incredibly busy that weekend so they settled on a lunch date at a café in the Place de la Sorbonne for the following Monday.

On the way home Blane was in seventh heaven. He had never dreamt of seeing Barbara again, let alone of having a lengthy conversation with her. He knew she was far above his sphere, yet she was affable and seemed to want to have a relationship. Obviously she could never take him seriously, but he was happy that at least she wanted to be friends.

Over the ensuing months Blane saw Barbara at every available moment. Since she was so busy with school, family and the theatre, this could usually be managed only at lunch. Blane also frequently attended her performances. He chalked this up to cultural *engagement* and happily accompanied her home.

They always had plenty to talk about. Their mutual interest in French literature and history meant that there was an endless succession of intellectual novelties to be discussed. Barbara enjoyed his companionship and frequently asked his advice when she wrote papers for her classes. Thus they grew in their affection for French culture and, it may be said, for each other. Blane dared not think where this might lead. He kept up his e-mail correspondence with Avery and did not raise his sights to a level to which he could not hope to aspire.

Nonetheless he found that he was changing. He had thought of himself as a teacher, but he was not sure whether he was more suited to the elementary or the secondary level. After he had clocked a lot of conversational time with Barbara, however, he began to think he was more suited to the college level. He thought he could be happy as a college professor.

And so it was that Blane metamorphosed imperceptibly over the winter into someone that Barbara would be more interested in and that possibly Avery would not. He wondered what Barbara's father was like, but she mentioned him seldom, and then only in a personal context, never in his professional pursuits. Blane realized after a while that Barbara had no idea of what her father did during working hours. She saw him only in the evening and on weekends. She rarely attended embassy parties, and when she did, it was purely in a social capacity. Blane thought she was closer to understanding her mother's position, a fact which endeared her to him more than ever, but still he did not aim higher.

When his parents visited at Easter, they whisked him away on a tour of southern France. Since there was no opportunity for them to meet Barbara, Blane decided to keep the relationship to himself. One day, when they were sitting in a sidewalk café in Saint-Tropez, his mother asked him in a casual voice if he had ever run into Barbara McMahon. Blane concentrated on the sailboats floating silently in and out of the harbor and replied offhandedly that he had seen her occasionally on campus.

"So why don't you speak to her?" his mother asked.

"I have," he answered. "She's really busy. I don't think she has a lot of extra time for someone like me."

His mother pondered this and said, "You're a lot more interesting fellow than you think, Blane," and then changed the subject. Blane was relieved, but in the few days of vacation that remained to them he caught her looking at him quizzically more than once. She did not return to the topic, however, and Blane was content. After all, why discuss something that was not?

In May the semester was drawing to a close, and Blane was too busy preparing for examinations to think of anything else. When the last exam was over, however, the full impact of leaving Paris hit him, and he felt depressed. He had arranged to meet Barbara for dinner as she was between acting engagements. He thought of it as a kind of farewell, but he had not yet told her that he would be flying home the next day. He went through the motions of packing, but his heart was not in it. He had been so happy in Paris, and now it was all coming to an end. He wondered how Barbara would react. Would she brush off their relationship as just another experience in life? Was her life so full that his portion of it might easily be taken up by other pursuits.? He knew she could participate more in embassy social life anytime she chose. He did not know why she had spent so much time with him anyway. Maybe she just wanted a fellow student to talk to. Now he felt devastated to think he was going to lose her. He even considered not showing up at *Chez Jacques*, but he could not bear to think of her disbelief and disappointment.

    At 6:30 p.m. he found himself seated at a table in the restaurant trying to dream up some felicitous topics of conversation. Barbara arrived a few minutes later, and they gave the waiter their order. She was ebullient, entertaining him with a humorous account of the amnesia she had temporarily experienced in her last exam with respect to Proust. When she finally recalled her notes, they were quite rearranged in her mind. She thought everything had come out okay in the exam book, however, and perhaps her answer was even somewhat novel in approach, which she imagined a graduate student marking a plethora of exams might appreciate.

    Blane listened contentedly. Barbara was euphoric. Summer was on the threshold, and she thought she would get a part in "Le Cid." That would be very demanding because there was so much to memorize and one had to bring alive an older concept of honor. Blane nodded in agreement. And so they progressed from topic to topic in a lighthearted fashion.

    It was during dessert that Blane sprang the bad news that he would be leaving the next day. She looked at him in shock, her fork suspended in mid-air.

"No!" she moaned.

"I waited to tell you because I was afraid you would be unhappy."

She had no reply to that, but he could see the tears welling up in her eyes. She put her fork down.

"Look, Barbara, if I could stay, I would, but I can't. There's a job waiting for me at home."

"I understand," she said, but her eyes were dismal ponds of blue. He was surprised that she felt so strongly.

"I'll keep in touch with you by e-mail," he promised. She nodded and looked away. She said she was not hungry and was feeling tired. Blane's mind was doing cartwheels as he struggled to find words to express the feelings he had never allowed himself to entertain before. He was not fast enough. She was already moving toward the door. Blane motioned to the waiter for the bill and, in his rush to quit the restaurant, left most of his money on the table. He maneuvered through the field of tables like a football player avoiding a tackle and gained the sidewalk, relieved to find that she was waiting for him there. They walked silently together toward the Metro. On the platform and in the train they spoke cursorily, and she looked absent-minded.

When they reached the embassy gate, Blane blurted out, "I have no prospects. I don't know my future. I have nothing to offer you. I don't even know what I am going to do in life. I care for you, but I cannot promise anything at this stage of the game. I don't want to make you miserable. Oh tell me you'll be happy! Don't be sad!"

"At least you are honest," she replied. "I appreciate that. What we have had was very precious, and perhaps we need to stand back a little from that experience now. They say absence makes the heart grow fonder."

Blane moved closer and said, "I never knew ... I never dreamt ..."

She gave him a sharp look. "Is there someone else?"

Blane stopped. His feelings were in turmoil. "Yes," he admitted in a low voice.

"I thought so. Otherwise you would never have been so slow. Come back when you are free. I will not share you with anyone else."

"I'll be in touch," he said.

"Adieu," she replied and left him.

High Society

Divine Providence was not a topic on which Eustacia Flynn could have discoursed for an impressive length of time. Indeed, she was fairly innocent of any particular familiarity with the subject. If she had been queried on the workings of that mysterious force, however, she would have said that, as a practical matter, a person should maintain good relations with the Deity and then trust what thoughts and nudges from the environment might occur. Although a theologian might have stated it differently, with arcane verbiage and sentences running well nigh unto paragraphs, he would probably have agreed that Eustacia had captured the essence of the matter. It must be confessed that she did not have immense quantities of experience to bring to bear on the question. She had not come up through the school of hard knocks, saved from imminent disasters by timely interventions of a fortuitous cast, but had, through no merit of her own, been born into an affectionate and affluent Dublin family and had somehow arrived at adulthood with a serene disposition and no worries aside from the usual difficulties of passing occasional spasms of university examinations. The relative peacefulness of her overall situation she attributed to the quiet workings of Divine Providence and not to any special strategy of her own.

    Be that as it may, in the course of her progress toward adulthood a certain eccentricity had developed in Eustacia's approach to her social ambience which had most peculiar consequences. This eccentricity derived from the fact that she had discovered at the tender age of sixteen that she was attractive to men. She knew this was true when she received five telephone calls in a single evening from young men requesting the honor of escorting her to a college dance. The rapid succession of the invitations made her feel fairly certain that there was some ulterior motive lurking behind them, and she had not reflected long before she thought that she had discovered what it was. Ever since her father had won the Nobel Prize for literature, her parents had become immensely popular at soirées, dinner parties and theatricals. Now the same phenomenon was occurring in her life. It was really the father the young men wanted to see, not the daughter. Having mulled this over, Eustacia decided not to attend the dance in question at all. In fact, she found she derived so much pleasure from rejecting invitations meant for her father that she decided never to date period. Since her parents took her along with them on weekends to social gatherings in and around Dublin, there was little prospect that her social life would suffer as a result of her decision.

    In her final undergraduate year at University College Dublin, Eustacia was living at home, from whence she had an easy commute to campus. It was all so convenient that she felt she had the best of all possible worlds. Her only problem in life was doing well in her studies. This was no mean feat since she was concentrating in French, Spanish and German simultaneously, frequently speaking all three in a single day.

Accompanying her parents to social affairs only on weekends kept Eustacia in circulation but did not compromise her academic progress. She envisaged herself as having both marriage and a career. For this reason she had taken St. Margaret of Scotland as her role model. She liked Queen Margaret because she had had a happy marriage and had fostered Christianity and culture in Scotland. While Eustacia felt reasonably certain that she would be getting married, she did not want to get involved with anyone just yet, and especially not with someone who was more interested in her father than in herself. She envisioned herself as going to graduate school and then, when her studies were over, taking men more seriously.

Thus it was that one Friday night in November Eustacia accompanied her parents to a soirée at the Shanahans. Shortly after their arrival she separated from the older set, as was her wont and joined her agemates. Soon they were babbling along happily together. Babbling along in company was their usual social interstice.

This mode of group sociability was in full swing when all of a sudden Eustacia became aware of a new face looking at her from the other side of the group. It belonged to a tall, dark and handsome man in his late twenties who was gazing at Eustacia in wonder. When he noticed her eyes on him, he smiled and said, "May I join you?"

"Of course," Eustacia had the grace to reply.

"Don't let me interrupt you," said the stranger.

"It was nothing. We were just tossing the bubble conversation around."

"Bubble conversation? Is that an Irish expression?"

"Heavens no! I just made it up. Where are you from?"

"Wittelstein."

"Oh! You have an American accent."

"My mother is an American."

Eustacia noticed that her friends had drifted away, and she and the stranger were left alone together in the crowd. Now that she had done a background check, she thought they might as well get acquainted.

"My name is Eustacia Flynn," she came to the point. "What's yours?"

"Johann."

With a certain sense of shock, Eustacia realized that her name had not lit up any recognition patterns in his mind. He was obviously not into the flurry of the Dublin literary scene. She thought, here I have a chance to have a normal conversation without any feeling that my father, and not myself, is the real attraction.

"So what brings a Wittelsteiner to Dublin?" she asked. "I should think we were a bit out of the way for you."

"Actually, I am here visiting a friend for the weekend."

A waiter with hors d'oeuvres happened by at this moment so they made a selection. Eustacia noticed that Johann kept his eyes locked on her and hardly remarked what he chose.

"You said you were visiting a friend."

"Yes, Gregory Byrnes. Do you know him?"

"Of course I know him. Everyone knows him. Gregory is very well-connected." Better connected than I am, she thought. "How do you know him?"

"We were friends at university."

"Not here in Dublin!"

"No, we met at the University of Geneva."

That showed him how well she knew Gregory.

"Oh, I thought there was something foreign about Gregory."

Just at that moment Gregory appeared and, smiling apologies, whisked his friend away. Esutacia chalked the conversation up to experience and looked around for her peer group.

An hour or two later, as she was preparing to leave, Johann reappeared.

"I'm so glad you are still here," he said. "I wonder if we could get together tomorrow for lunch."

"I don't date," Eustacia blurted out without thinking. His face fell. She thought, since he doesn't know who my father is, perhaps I should make an exception.

"May I ask why?" he inquired, a slightly pained expression on his face.

"I just found I was attracting too much attention so I put a stop to it."

"Oh, so you have that problem too." He relaxed and paused to consider his next move. Eustacia waited, curious to know what he would say next. This conversation was taking a surprising turn.

"Then when can I see you again?" he asked. It was a simple question simply put.

"Well, my parents are giving a reception next Saturday. You and Gregory are welcome to come if you like."

He took down the address carefully.

"I suppose there is no chance you will be appearing in public before then."

"Tomorrow night we are going to a dinner party at the Flannerys."

Eustacia's father was approaching, and Johann melted away. When Eustacia thought it over later, she felt that he was probably not a crook trying to avoid detection but had simply recognized the paternal look and had decided to avoid complications. The fact that he had evinced no particular interest in her father was a plus with Eustacia. He does not know, she thought. He likes me for myself.

Eustacia thought no more about her new acquaintance so it was with some measure of surprise that she discovered him at the Flannerys the following evening beaming at her from across the room. Then she saw Gregory Byrnes over his shoulder and realized how he had gained entrée. He walked over to join her.

"Congratulations!" she greeted him. "I see you are well-connected in Dublin society."

"Gregory is well-connected," he corrected her. "I just tag along as you do."

She nodded, a little nonplussed. Had he found out about her father? At least he knew that the family was well-connected, but then, of course, everyone at the Flannerys was well-connected.

He saw that he had disconcerted her so he changed the subject.

"Can you recommend any sightseeing I might undertake in Dublin without the favor of your company?"

She did not know how to respond. Perhaps she should lift the injunction against dating since he was a foreigner and had no interest in her father.

"I am embarrassing you. Forgive me. Do you mind a little friendly banter?"

Thus the conversation proceeded and soon Eustacia was thoroughly enjoying herself.

She was surprised again when the time came for everyone to sit down at table because she was seated next to Johann. Gregory had apparently managed everything. He had even managed to place himself down the table out of earshot.

Conversation with Johann was light and easy. Somewhere between the first and second courses she found herself telling him about her German literature classes and the paper she was writing on Goethe. He had a few opinions about the sage of Weimar and at one point forgetfully digressed into German. She found herself answering in that tongue and so they, in effect, had a private conversation in a public place.

"I say, Eustacia," protested Harold Winchester, an elderly gentleman seated on her left, at the end of dinner, "you have been neglecting me all evening."

"Oh, I'm sorry," she said. "And just for that I will not neglect you now." She smiled and nodded to Johann and then walked away arm-in-arm with her old friend.

On the way home her father wanted to know who the young man was she had been talking to.

"I talked to many people," she replied nonchalantly.

"I mean the one at dinner," her father persisted. "Who was he?"

"Some fellow named Johann who is visiting Gregory Byrnes. In fact, I invited the two of them to come to our reception next Saturday, but I have no idea whether or not they will actually make it."

Her father's interest in the subject subsided, and Eustacia was glad she had minimized the importance of her encounter with Johann. Why should her father know everything? Besides, she might never see him again. It was too early for gossip.

Johann started turning up every weekend, but managed to circulate so well that his interest in Eustacia was not especially remarked. Her father had seemingly forgotten him. Eustacia guessed that Gregory Byrnes' friendship vouched sufficiently for the Wittelsteiner.

Christmas arrived, classes were out, and Johann was a thousand kilometers away. He had said he had too many social engagements in Wittelstein to come to Dublin over the holidays. Eustacia was working on papers so, between her assignments and the whirlwind of parties, she hardly missed him. Whenever the thought of him came to mind, she resolutely put it on hold. She had known him too briefly to spend any serious thinking time on the relationship, but one rainy afternoon she found herself consulting an atlas in the library to ascertain the exact location of Wittelstein.

Nonetheless Johann had largely vanished from her thoughts when he showed up at a soirée on the weekend after New Year's. Eustacia was surprised at how happy she was to see him.

"Oh, Johann, we have missed you so!" she gushed.

He gave her a penetrating look. "I am glad to hear it. I missed you too." Then he turned to admire the Christmas decorations which were still in place. She had a wonderful time that evening, but afterwards she did not allow herself to think about her emotions because classes were starting up again, and all other thoughts had to be shelved.

In the spring term she chose mostly German literature courses. She thought that as long as Johann was around, she might as well seize the opportunity to perfect her German and expand her knowledge of the literature. *Carpe diem*, she thought.

And so she continued to see him on weekends. By now their tête-à-têtes were conducted mostly German. Although this afforded them some privacy, Eustacia noticed that Johann was careful to keep the conversation social and not personal. It seemed like an ingrained habit with him. He apparently assumed that someone was listening.

To Eustacia's chagrin, Johann did not come to Dublin for the Easter weekend, claiming that family and other commitments required his presence in Wittelstein. He felt he did not have the option of nonattendance.

The following weekend, however, he returned, and this time he seemed somewhat pensive. Eustacia was oblivious to his mood. She was exuberant over being accepted in the doctoral program in Comparative Literature, although Johann appeared singularly unimpressed when she told him.

"What? Aren't you happy for my success?" she asked.

"Yes, of course I am happy," he replied with a scowl. "You deserve it." Then he was silent, and Eustacia felt odd. She dropped the subject and went on to something she knew would interest him.

After final examinations there was a round of graduation parties. At a dinner dance at the Royal Marine Hotel on the southern tip of Dublin Bay Eustacia floated through a couple of waltzes with Johann. He danced in so courtly a manner that Eustacia could easily imagine herself in the swirl of a Viennese ball. When the music ended, they walked among the terraces and found a bench to rest on. They were overlooking Dublin Bay amid magnolias shimmering in the moonlight. Eustacia felt immersed in poetry.

"Eustacia," Johann was speaking gently to her in English. "This is a lovely evening and a wonderful occasion, but perhaps it is time that we come to some sort of understanding."

"I like understandings," she said, amenable to the direction the conversation was taking.

That gave him a little encouragement. "We have a terrific friendship, and I am hoping that it can become something more."

"Yes," she replied.

"I love you, Eustacia. Will you marry me?"

"I love you too, Johann." The words rushed out. "But how can we marry when your life is in Wittelstein and mine is in Dublin?"

"Then I am asking you, for love, to become *daheim* in Wittelstein. You would fit in well back home, Eustacia. My parents and my brothers would love you. The people …" He trailed off.

Eustacia saw her dreams collapsing and obeyed an impulse. "How can I leave Dublin when I have been accepted in a doctoral program? I have been working for three years to reach this point. How can I abandon my studies just when I am succeeding?"

"I can't answer that, Eustacia. As my wife, you would have to live in Wittelstein."

She did not know how to reply. "I will think it over" was all she said, and that was where they left it.

Graduation was a dream fulfilled. Eustacia listened attentively to the commencement speakers and drank in all their idealistic prose. At the same time, in the back of her mind she mulled over Johann's proposal. She wanted to say yes, but she was reluctant to give up the thought of obtaining her doctorate. She wondered what St. Margaret would have done. She would have married, of course, but she had not wanted to go to graduate school.

On the following weekend they met at an evening affair hosted by the O'Malleys. Strolling about the house, they found an unoccupied window seat in an alcove and claimed it. Johann asked if she had come to a decision and she answered in the negative. He said, "Let's discuss it. Why do you want to study comparative literature?"

"Because my father is a writer. I want to be conversant in literature."

"Your father is a writer? He must be a rather successful one, to judge by the style in which he keeps you."

"Yes," she admitted. "If you were more interested in literature, you would have heard of him."

"I must confess I have not done a lot of reading outside of politics and economics," he said. Then after a pause he added, "So you want to be a writer like your father."

"Yes," she admitted. It was her secret wish, one she had never told a living soul. Yet Johann had guessed it.

"You can do that in Wittelstein. That goes perfectly well with being a wife and mother. And if you should want

42

to study German literature, you would find plenty of opportunities in Wittelstein. We have an excellent library. You would even find enough to read in French and English. You don't need a doctorate to be a writer."

Eustacia had to admit this was true. She felt a rush of emotion. "Yes," she said. "Yes, yes, yes, I will marry you." Other guests were walking by so they sealed their bargain with a handshake.

"Now that we are engaged," Johann grinned, "would you go out with me on a date?"

"Yes, yes, yes," she breathed. She loved saying the word.

"Eustacia, come home with me. You can meet my parents and find out what Wittelstein is like."

"I would love to," she replied, and so it was settled. At some point in the subsequent conversation she inquired as to what flight they would be taking.

"I have my own plane," he answered.

"Oh my! I had no idea."

"There are many things you have no idea of, my dear."

And so it was that two days later Eustacia found herself on the tarmac boarding a private jet. Johann helped her get installed in the aircraft and then turned his attention to the controls. They took off under sunny skies and had an uneventful flight during which he pointed out to her the sights below. Eustacia was thrilled. Within a couple of hours they approached Zurich International Airport. Johann landed the plane and taxied over to the terminal. Once they were inside, he headed toward a special checkpoint where the customs official smiled at him and waved him through. "The lady is with me," Johann declared. The agent smiled again and waved Eustacia through.

"That was nice," she murmured to him as they left the building.

"I have a diplomatic passport," he replied.

Just then a man in uniform approached to take their luggage. "Welcome back, Your Highness," he said.

Transcendence

      While he was growing up, Valerian Manning had attended a few lectures on the necessity of going beyond one's own concerns in order to experience tranquility and joy. This meant sloughing off egocentric considerations and acting to benefit others. Speakers invariably claimed that if a person transcended his own narrowly-construed interests and acted to enhance the lives of others, Euphoria would result. As a consequence, Valerian thought he should be on the lookout for opportunities to augment the happiness of others and thereby his own personal sense of well-being. It was only later that he came to appreciate that this dynamic represented reality for only some of his acquaintances and that many other people lived according to instinct and power concerns and easily misconstrued acts of benevolence as self-interested.
      Valerian had grown up in a time of great peace and prosperity when many people acted out their concern for their neighbors and, as a result, a feeling of general euphoria ensued. In his community liberal views and gracious manners held sway. His parents had purchased a

home in a quiet, woodland neighborhood on the outskirts of Sophia, a city-state whose residents held allegiance to a mystical light that emanated from its center. Once a week they flocked to bask in this mysterious light which was alleged to have a civilizing influence on its beholders, enabling them to transcend their egos and access serenity and joy. In fact, basking in the light was a condition for citizenship in Sophia. Occasionally residents of the city traveled abroad, sometimes to other cities where the same light prevailed, sometimes to Kratos where only hints of the light were to be found. People who dwelt in Kratos also came to Sophia for sightseeing or immigrated there to be nearer to the light.

Valerian lived close to the border between Sophia and Kratos. In fact, he was well-acquainted with the customs of Kratos because he had gone to elementary and secondary school there. Since most children in his neighborhood went to school in Sophia, Valerian did not know them very well except for Mary Halloran who lived next door. This is probably why, when the time came for Valerian to go to college, he decided to go to a university in Kratos. His grandfather had objected, observing that there were excellent universities in Sophia and, if he wanted to study abroad, there were plenty of topnotch universities in other cities. In short, it was not necessary to go to college in Kratos. Since his parents discounted his grandfather's views, Valerian applied to Technical University in Kratos without a second thought. He was elated when he was accepted and felt that he would make many friends there.

Friends meant a lot to Valerian. When he did things for his friends and spent time with them, he would have a "peak experience." There as no gainsaying it. Friendship was a high for Valerian. The light in Sophia had once been a high for him too, but since he visited it only on weekends with his parents, it did not dominate his thinking, and he did not miss it when he left for Technical University.

Probably the main reason why Valerian did not miss the light was the fact that his grandfather was praying for him. Every morning he would awaken to happy thoughts and thoughts of his grandfather. This euphoria would sometimes recur at other times of the day, and consequently Valerian harbored kind thoughts with respect to his forebear.

Generally speaking, traffic between Sophia and Kratos moved back and forth with no difficulty. Whenever the school bus went through Sophian customs, the agents smiled and waved to the young people. That was why when war broke out, it was such a shock to Valerian.

Sophia had been losing citizens steadily for several decades. People were restive under the rule that they had to bathe in the light once a week. They felt it was unnecessary; it seemed to make no difference in their lives. They thought they would enjoy life more in Kratos where there was a continual round of parties and more relaxed mores in general. Even Valerian could see the advantages of the easygoing lifestyle that characterized Kratos. At first, when he went to Technical University, he kept to the ascetic customs of Sophia, but gradually he began to immerse himself in the Kratos way of life. He knew he was getting farther from the light and what was purported to be its humanizing and civilizing influence, but he still felt euphoric on account of his grandfather's prayers so he figured things were all right. That is why the war came as such a shock.

Valerian was in his last semester as an undergraduate at Technical University and had been admitted to its medical school for the fall term when events took an untoward turn. He could remember afterwards exactly where he was when the news came. He had been disco dancing with friends on a Saturday night in a dimly-lit lounge at the student union. He was busy doing his usual wobble to the throbbing music when suddenly the band stopped playing and someone took the microphone to announce that the Kratos army had just mounted an assault on Sophia. The lights went up, and Valerian and his friends gathered around a television set to listen to the news. A jubilant anchorman was reporting that there had been some casualties among the Sophian border guards and customs officials as the Kratos army occupied the borderlands and advanced into a couple of suburbs. Valerian's friends cheered. He realized with surprise and consternation that he was the only one who was traumatized by the news. On the contrary, his friends were clapping each other on the back and laughing and boasting about how their arm would defeat Sophia and overrun it. Valerian felt like the wind had been knocked out of him. These were his friends, but they were laughing about the demise of the customs agents he had waved to as a child. Valerian made his excuses and returned to his room.

All the next day he sat tensely in front of a television set in a lounge in the student union. The news was not good. There were further casualties, and diplomatic relations had been severed. The Sophian army had regrouped and struck back, recovering some lost territory. Valerian visited the library to pore over a map of Sophia. His parents' home was fairly close to the action, but their suburb had not been overrun.

It was while watching television at noon on Monday that Valerian heard some distressing news that impelled him to drop out of classes for the rest of the day. His grandfather's name topped the list of Sophian casualties. It seemed that the old man had been out for his morning constitutional and had been picked off by sniper fire from an advance patrol of the Kratos army. Valerian stared grimly into the void while all around him his friends were rejoicing over the Sophian casualties.

Someone called out, "Look at Sophie! He looks like he's in another world."

"What planet are *you* living on, Sophie?" cried a dessicated voice.

"What's the matter? Don't you have the stomach for war?" They circled him like vultures.

Valerian looked at them. "My grandfather ..." He broke off, tears in his eyes.

After a pause a young woman commented, "His grandfather must have been among the casualties." Valerian nodded his assent.

"Sorry," someone ventured. "Sorry," many of them echoed.

Valerian realized they were attempting to be sympathetic. He grimaced a smile and walked away, trying to hide his tears.

"That's what you get for coming from the enemy," someone called after him.

"Hey, there's more news," another said, and they turned back to the television, happy to forget about Valerian.

The next morning Valerian awoke at 6:00 a.m. as usual, but there was no euphoria. He went through the day attending classes and watching the television news for the latest from the front. A battle was going on, and the casualties were mounting. The government called for the support of its citizens, and patriotic rallies against Sophia were being held on campus and all over Kratos. Valerian felt like the protagonist in a Greek tragedy. His friends were excited by the war, but he felt as if he had been struck in the solar plexus, and there was no relief in sight. His euphoria had died with his grandfather. Valerian walked around lost in his thoughts, aware that people were not talking to him unless he initiated the conversation. He knew relationships in Kratos depended on reciprocity, and he was not doing enough to tap into friendly outcomes. Final examinations were imminent so Valerian decided to stick his head in the books and get back to socializing during the summer session when he would be taking some psychology courses.

The day after his examinations were over Valerian grabbed a few necessities and jumped on a train headed toward Sophia. He wondered how he would cross the borderlands now that they had become a battleground. As he pondered this dilemma, he prayed to his grandfather to show him the way. Then he remembered Ollie, one of his classmates in high school. Ollie lived on a Kratos farm adjacent to the border. A path led from the rear of his property through a woods to Sophia, coming out a few kilometers from the home of Valerian's parents. Valerian had used it once or twice. Happy in this thought, he decided to set his course toward Ollie's place.

Sitting by himself in the train, Valerian tried to read a book, but he could not forget the cold. There was a distinct chill in the air, but more than that, the people were cold too. He thought that perhaps it had always been cool or cold in Kratos; he had just not noticed it. His previous contact with the light as well as his grandfather's prayers had kept him warm. Now they were gone, and Valerian felt the cold. He started reminiscing about his grandfather, and these thoughts warmed him slightly, but the cold remained perceptible both in the atmosphere and in the people. The loud, strident voices of some women sitting nearby grated on his ears. The guffaws of some men discussing the impending conquest of Sophia sent another chill through his system. He tried not to listen, but that was impossible. And still the cold came.

It was twilight when the train finally approached Trader's Notch, the last stop in Kratos before the tracks led to Sophian customs. Now, on account of the war, Trader's Notch was the terminus for all trains. Valerian placed a call to Ollie on his cellphone and asked him to meet the train. A few minutes later the train slowed to a halt, and Valerian alit on the busy platform. Soldiers were milling around in the station so Valerian decided to stand unobtrusively against the wall. Eventually Ollie arrived in a farm truck, beaming a welcome, and Valerian climbed in.

"Ollie, am I glad to see you!" he exclaimed.

"So you're home for the summer?" Ollie asked as they drove off.

"No, just for a few weeks. Then I have to go back for the summer session. Say, Ollie, I couldn't figure out how to get across the borderlands until I remembered the path at the rear of your property."

"Oho!" said Ollie. "That's the perfect route. You should be safe from patrols there. They are looking for the enemy in open country, not in the woods."

"They shot my grandfather…. They killed him, Ollie."

"He must have been in the wrong place at the wrong time because they don't go after civilians. They just go after the military."

Valerian pondered this one for a while. Then he decided to change the subject. "So what have you been up to lately, Ollie?" he asked.

"Just planting wheat and corn and tending vegetables. Oh yes! I volunteered for the army."

"You volunteered? So when will you be going?"

"Any day now. I'm just waiting to hear from them. I want to contribute to the war effort and help put an end to that crazy myth about some light in the center of Sophia."

"What myth, Ollie? There really is a light in the center of Sophia, a mystical light."

"Oh come on now. That's a lot of hogwash. You can't believe that."

"I do."

"Well, that's just dumb. We have to free you people from that way of thinking so that you can live according to reason the way we do."

They turned off the road onto a dirt track that led to the perimeter of the farm.

"If Pops heard you talking like that," Ollie continued, "he'd be calling the cops for sure."

Valerian had no comment. He knew Ollie was doing him a big favor.

"Once we defeat the Sophian army, you will see the error of your ways."

Valerian felt uncertain about how to reply and said nothing. They rode along in silence for a couple of minutes. Then Ollie pulled up.

"Well, here we are. The path starts over there. I think you can find your way in the moonlight."

"Ollie, you are a great friend," Valerian said. "I will always be grateful to you for this. I suppose I can come through here again in three weeks if the border isn't open by then."

"Sure. My old man will give you a lift to town if I'm not around, but don't talk to him about no mystical light."

"Okay, I promise," Valerian said and he swung down from the truck. He had located the path and was about to plunge into the woods when he heard Ollie call out behind him, "Oh, and Val, say hello to Rafe and Bertie for me."

"I will, Ollie," Valerian called back and disappeared into the woods.

The path was seldom used and difficult to discern even by day so Valerian had to guide himself more by his sense of direction than by anything else. A full moon hung benevolently over the woodland, aiding him as he stepped gingerly around twigs that might crackle and signal his presence to any scout from Kratos who might be in the vicinity. He breathed more easily when at last he saw a couple of houses through the trees. The worst was over, and he was safe in Sophia again. He gained the road and kept to it, stepping up the pace as he did not want to set off any dog alarms. He decided not to use his cellphone to contact his parents as he did not want any possible Kratos sharpshooters in the vicinity to know his whereabouts.

It was around midnight when he finally saw the familiar outline of his parents' home emerging from among the trees. The moonlight dropped a hazy nostalgia over the red colonial house, and Valerian could almost imagine himself again as a child playing out in front. He was still toying with this thought as he rang the doorbell. After a long minute a light went on in the house, and shortly thereafter his father answered the door in his bathrobe, expressing surprise and thankfulness that Valerian was safely home. His mother heard his voice and came downstairs to embrace him. Valerian thought they both looked well and somehow happier than he remembered them. The three of them wandered into the family room and settled into some comfortable chairs for a chat. Valerian's eyes fell on the bookshelves lining the walls where, among other things, the beloved books of his youth nestled, and a fresh wave of emotion inundated him. His mother brought in some refreshments and Valerian told them what had occurred in Kratos. Then his father commented on the eulogies at his grandfather's wake and funeral. Unbeknownst to the family, his grandfather had been a member of the Praetorian Guards, a status that merited an honor guard at the obsequies. His parents had been duly impressed.

Valerian's father then proceeded to discuss the war. "It hasn't really affected us here," he said, "although sometimes we hear the sound of guns."

"I take it that the Kratos military is adhering to the Ares Convention and abstaining from aerial bombing."

"Yes, they don't want to destroy our art treasures. Since those are scattered among the general populace, we are well protected.

"Ollie says the light is just a myth. He wants to eliminate our army and then re-educate us so we won't believe in the light anymore.

"They will have a hard time doing that," his father answered. "There really is a light in Sophia, and too many people around here have personal experience of it." His mother nodded her assent.

Valerian was surprised at the tone of conviction in his father's voice. More had changed than he had originally thought.

It was too late at night to call anyone, but the next day he got in touch with his neighbor Mary Halloran. After thay had exchanged some pleasantries, he asked if she would like to get together for dinner some evening. Mary was not too interested.

"Thank you," she replied, "but I have to tell you that while you were away, I became engaged to Raphael Blythe. We are going to a lecture and social at Sophia University on Friday night, and if you would like to tag along, we would be glad to have you."

"You and Rafe are engaged?" Valerian was surprised.

"Yes, we were interested in each other for a while, but we just met at social gatherings so no one suspected our secret. Then he finally popped the question in March and we went public."

"Well, that's terrific. Congratulations!" And so the matter was settled. Valerian would accompany them to the lecture.

He spent the next few days going to all his usual haunts and visiting the light. The light ... Valerian had forgotten what a wonderful experience it was to bask in the light. There was some ineffable quality emanating from it. It was luminous, yet it never hurt the beholder's eyes. It was a spiritual experience, Valerian thought, and he was loath to walk away from it.

On Friday night Raphael and Mary picked him up in an old jalopy, and together they drove to the university. The lecture was being held in a Gothic edifice that boasted an auditorium with a high-beamed ceiling and wood-paneled walls hung with the escutcheons of affiliated universities flaunting mottos such as "Lux et Veritas," "Semper Fidelis," "Annuit Coeptis" and others. The auditorium was only half full when they arrived so they left their jackets on some seats close to the podium and circulated around the hall. Raphael introduced Valerian to a knot of people with whom they had a lively exchange. The lights began to dim, and they returned to their seats to listen to the lecture.

The speaker's comments went by Valerian; he was too busy trying to sort out the people he had just met. Carefully he reviewed faces and tidbits of conversation, oblivious to the eminent lecturer on the stage. When the talk was over, Valerian plunged anew into the social whirl.

At the end of the evening Valerian felt the euphoria of a group for the first time since the war started. The magic of friendship was working for him in Sophia also.

During his vacation Valerian visited the light several times and met with his new friends. Slowly a new idea began to take shape in his mind. Nonetheless, he had not proceeded far with this reflection when the three weeks of vacation were over and it was time to return to Technical University for the summer session. He did not want to leave the light, but he thought he would be able to maintain a feeling of well-being if he meditated on it. He knew also that his parents would pray for him and so he thought that everything would be fine.

The war was at a standstill. The Sophian military had pushed the Kratos force back to the borderlands. People expected a truce any day. The diplomats were talking peace. The news returned to normal. Valerian did not know if Ollie was still at home because communications with Kratos were severed.

On the night of his return, Valerian's parents drove him at three o'clock in the morning to the place where the path began. They hugged and kissed; Valerian thought he detected tears in his mother's eyes.

"Come home soon, son," his father said.

"I'll be home before you know it," Valerian replied and then resolutely set his face towards the woods and what lay beyond it.

The woods were silent. A half moon hung over the trees like a smouldering lantern. It was enough. Valerian could see traces of the path. He thought about the mystery of the light and how it melted those who contemplated it so they became kinder and more gentle. It erased barriers between people. Valerian wondered about the origins of the light. He had to confess he did not understand it; he only recognized its ineffable presence. He pitied the people who did not know about it.

A shot rang out, and a nearby twig broke off. Valerian instinctively dropped to the ground. More shots splintered twigs and ripped bark from the trees around him. Valerian thought he detected glints of steel ahead of him and to the right. There were enemy sharpshooters in the woods. He jumped up and fled back along the path, hoping the trees would cover his retreat. Shots whizzed past him as he raced through the woods back to the safety of the well-kept lawns of Sophia. He heard men crashing through the underbrush behind him and prayed he would elude them. Suddenly the roofs of the nearest houses in Sophia loomed up ahead, inspiring him to manage an extra burst of speed. He gained the clearing and put a few houses between him and his adversaries. Then he stopped, gasping for breath and straining to catch any sound coming from the woods. A dog started barking, and Valerian began sprinting down the road toward home, keeping up a steady pace as if the danger were still imminent. His thoughts were in turmoil as he tried to make sense of what had occurred.

At length he saw the familiar abode and made a last spurt, feeling like the exhausted runner arriving in Athens with the news from Marathon. He pressed the doorbell wildly, and in no time his father appeared in his pajamas to admit him.

Valerian rushed inside, slammed the door shut and bolted it and exclaimed to his astounded father, "We have to call Central Defense immediately! The Kratos army is massing in the woods!"

The Desert

Father Jeremy O'Faolain was a happy man. He had been a priest for 31 years and was grateful for every minute of it. As he looked out his office window at the postage-stamp rectory garden, he smiled to think how God had blessed him. Oh there had been ups and downs, but the good times had been more plentiful than the bad and more memorable.

Jeremy had come from a devout family. His father was a Son of St. Patrick and his mother a Daughter of St. Bridget at St. Columban parish, with the concomitant responsibilities accruing to these affiliations. Moreover, his mother had stayed up into the wee hours of the night doing chores and praying for everyone she knew and a lot of people she did not know. She prayed for everyone who was in trouble, and she prayed for everyone who was not in trouble in the hope that they would not get into trouble. That about covered the world, which was why she was so long about her prayers.

That was why when Jeremy announced one day at age 12 that he wanted to become a priest, his parents took it as a blessing. They thought his prayers would certainly keep the whole neighborhood out of trouble for a considerable interval of time.

And that was why also when Jeremy began to experience wakefulness in his mid-forties, he thought nothing of it. In fact, he was delighted to turn out to be like his mother and to have so many extra hours in the day to read, write and pray. He thought wakefulness was in the family and was a good thing.

Jeremy had been a seminary professor until recently. Then one day after teaching Church history for 30 years, he thought he had had enough. It was time for a change. He followed up this inspiration by seeing the rector at his earliest convenience about arranging for another assignment. So he felt no trepidation when the chancery called and invited him in for a chat.

"What did you have in mind?" Father Eustace Hale had asked him.

"Oh, I didn't have anything in particular in mind. I would be happy to take whatever you think best," Jeremy had replied diplomatically.

"I see," Eustace Hale had answered in measured tones. "Well, we have an opening at St. John of the Cross in Lost Valley. The pastor there has just retired, and the position hasn't been filled yet. A young curate is holding the fort."

"Lost Valley? Isn't that out in farm country?"

"Yes, it is. That's what's available if you want to be a pastor."

"Okay, I'll take it," Jeremy had replied. It was a bit far away, certainly a long drive from the center of things, but beggars can't be choosers, and so he was content. When he reflected on it afterwards, he thought the chancery had assigned him to a "safe" parish out in the countryside where he could do little harm.

In fact, he found that Lost Valley, complete with a state prison and a nursing home, was a pleasant, if busy, assignment. St. John of the Cross had an expandable workload, and he had had to be selective as to his activities or else the parish would run him and not he the parish. He had a worthy backup man in Father Noel Chandler, a 34-year-old priest he had met a few years back in Age of Faith and then again in Reformation and Counter Reformation. There was a bit of role reversal going on for a while as Noel taught him the ropes, but now he had found his legs and could manage for himself.

He had an appointment at 11:30 with George Bruhn. George was a retired engineer who had lost his wife several years ago. Jeremy had met him in prison ministry but did not know him on a personal basis.

George was on time and came to the point.

"Father, I don't know if you can help me with this, but I am at a loss to know how to deal with it on my own so I hope you will have a solution."

"Shoot," said Jeremy.

"Father, a few years back I was wakeful and not at all sleepy at night. Midnight would roll around, and I was still busy reading or listening to the radio. Then one night I got to thinking that maybe I should be sleeping so I turned out the light and tried to get some shuteye. After I had done this a few times, I stopped being wakeful and fell into a state of frequent drowsiness. I don't mean that I am drowsy during the day, but I am definitely drowsy at night. I can't sit down after supper without falling asleep."

Jeremy was surprised by this outburst. He did not know what to make of it. He could tell from the distressed look on George's face that something was terribly wrong, but he did not know what the solution might be.

"Oh!" he said. "And what did you think to do about it?"

"I came across something like it in the biography of St. Catherine of Bologna. In fact, it seemed to me that the exact same thing had happened to her."

"So what did she do about it?" Jeremy inquired.

"She prayed at night with her arms outstretched so as to keep from falling asleep. Finally, one day she heard angels singing, and she was cured of her drowsiness."

"A happy ending!" exclaimed Jeremy. "I have a distinct preference for happy endings. So did you try it?"

"Yes, I tried it a little but apparently not long enough because I didn't get to a solution."

"Oh!" Jeremy's face fell. Then he remembered something. "St. Dominic was quite an athlete late at night. While he prayed, he stood, he prostrated himself, he sat, he prayed with his arms upstretched and outstretched. Doubtless this kept him busy and therefore awake."

"That sounds interesting," said George. "I will have to try that. I wish I had accepted the state of wakefulness with grace. As it was, I thought I was abnormal."

"No, you are not abnormal." Jeremy felt he was on safe ground here. "It is quite normal for people to be wakeful as they grow older. God is simply giving them more time to do things like pray and read and write."

The conversation drifted into other channels. When the Angelus bell rang, they were busy discussing St. John of the Cross and his appreciation of the desert experience. Jeremy was enjoying the conversation so much that he invited George to stay for lunch. It was Noel's day off, and Jeremy thought it would be more fun to dine with conversation than to dine with a book.

George accepted and the two men proceeded to the dining room where the cook awaited them.

"Mrs. Pritchard, we're having company for lunch."

"Very good, Father. What will it be?"

"I'll have shrimp salad, fruit punch and apple sauce. What will you have, George? Use your imagination. We probably have it."

"Veggies and water, please."

Jeremy could see that George was not endowed with an excess of imagination with respect to culinary delights.

"What are you, some kind of vegetarian?" Jeremy smiled, but he felt he was being one-upped by a Desert Father.

George shook his head. "No, only on Fridays."

Jeremy relaxed. "Very well. Thank you, Mrs. Pritchard."

She disappeared and the two men resumed their conversation. An hour later they parted company, Jeremy to make a sick call and George to consult with a friend in prison ministry.

That evening Jeremy thought over what George had said. He thanked God and his mother that he had never thought of wakefulness in a negative light. He admired the man's ascetic attitude toward culinary delights, however. He reflected on his own alimentary experience. His mother had rustled up nutritious meals without managing to challenge the chefs of four-star restaurants. Seminary cuisine was down a peg from home cooking, but Jeremy had never been tempted to skip a meal. Only one member of the faculty had been a vegetarian, and he taught Christian Mystics. With a class like that, abstemious eating was probably an occupational hazard. Jeremy decided to put the whole idea on the back burner.

A week later he was alone for lunch as usual. The Angelus bell rang and, murmuring his prayers, he began moving in the direction of the dining room. Mrs. Pritchard was waiting for him.

"What will it be, Father?" she inquired.

"I'd just like some veggies and water, thank you," he replied.

* * * * *

A couple of months passed by before Jeremy saw George Bruhn again. It was at a parish lecture on the writings of Benedict XVI by Father Jacek Karski, a seminary professor who had traipsed out to Lost Valley for friendship's sake. All the parish movers and shakers as well as the daily Massgoers and a few souls Jeremy did not recognize were in attendance. In the question period that followed the lecture George Bruhn stood up and asked Father Karski about Benedict's mysticism. The seminary professor fielded this high pop fly by saying that the evidence for such had to be inferred from his writings.

The Daughters of St. Paula presided over the refreshments after the lecture, and Jeremy circulated among the movers and shakers and the daily Massgoers and even met some souls he did not recognize. The crowd was thinning out when George Bruhn approached him.

"Did you notice I was gone, Father?" he asked. Jeremy nodded. "I was out in California visiting my daughter. I just got back and I am sure glad I didn't miss this lecture. We should have more like it."

Jeremy agreed, wondering how many of his seminary buddies would be able to find Lost Valley on the map. Seeing that the remnants of the crowd were at a safe distance, he inquired offhandedly, "Whatever happened in that matter you mentioned to me?"

"You mean my propensity to fall asleep at the drop of a hat. Out in San Francisco I went to an all-night vigil in a church and have been fairly wakeful ever since. I don't spend a lot of time sitting down when I am alone because I have noticed that sitting down makes me fall asleep. I am a regular jack-in-the-box, what with popping up out of sedentary positions."

"The Lord has a sense of humor," Jeremy opined.

"My sense of what is going on is that I am not to take the tiller but let God steer the boat. In this case, He wants me standing, kneeling or moving around but not sitting down."

"That sounds like the Lord," responded Jeremy as they rejoined the fading crowd.

The Christmas Orphan

It was three o'clock in the afternoon on Christmas Eve, and Dr. Thomas Hanley was coming off his shift at the hospital. He changed into civilian clothes and was walking through a trifle of falling snow across town to the flower shop district on Sixth Avenue. Ducking into the first shop he found, he purchased an ebullient scarlet poinsettia that he thought would be expressive of his gratitude to his hostess that evening. He had no idea what Clarissa Bates' mother's taste was in flowers, but he thought that a poinsettia at Christmas would find a niche in any woman's heart.

Clarissa was in his Tuesday evening choral group, otherwise known as the Metropolitan Chorus. When she heard that he and Bill Sutherland, another chorister, were Christmas orphans, she invited them to visit her parents in the country for the holiday. Since Tom could not take off more than Christmas Day, it was impossible for him to fly home to visit his parents in California. Having nowhere else to go, he thought he would take a chance and accept the invitation. Clarissa was a nice girl, and he knew Bill could always be counted on to hold up his end of the conversation.

The plan was that he and Bill would go out to New Jersey on Christmas Eve for overnight and then return to New York sometime after dinner the following day. Tom had packed a travel bag with a few small gifts and had taken it to work that morning. Thus he strode along Sixth Avenue in the direction of Penn Station encumbered with a suitcase, a briefcase and now, a poinsettia plant.

He rendezvoused with Bill at the information booth in the train station. His friend immediately guessed the contents of his package. "Not a poinsettia!" he exclaimed. "How conventional can you get!"

"It was all I could think of," Tom replied. "What did you get Clarissa's mother?"

"Some chocolates."

"How unconventional!" Tom riposted sardonically.

They chatted a few more minutes before Clarissa appeared. She shepherded them onto a train full of people accoutered with traveling bags and large packages, and shortly thereafter they were whisked away to the provinces.

Clarissa's brother-in-law Joe met them with a broad grin at the Far Hills train station and drove them down snowy country lanes until at last they turned into a driveway leading to a rambling old house. A blanket of snow had obscured the outlines of the house so that in the enveloping darkness Tom could not discern its architecture. The white overlay had rendered it nondescript.

In the foyer Clarissa performed the introductions. There were, besides her father Gresham and her mother Irene, her sister Frossie (short for Euphrosyne) and her two children, Virgil and Horace, whose ages were in the single digits. This was to be the company for the evening and Tom believed that the nature of the occasion and the sociability of his hosts would prove a lively substitute for Christmas at home.

It was only when he stepped into the living room that he was able to discern the character of the house. It was a mansion dating from the exuberance of the 1920s. Everywhere there were shelves full of books. A bust of Julius Caesar was prominently displayed on a table along the wall. Irene admired the poinsettia that Tom had brought and placed it by a Nativity set on a table at the far end of the living room. The candy she received more dubiously, putting it away "for the children." Then she absented herself in the kitchen.

Tom and Bill were guided to their rooms by a loquacious Virgil who was full of speculation concerning what Santa might bring. Having been previously unaware of the existence of Virgil, Tom realized that he was not going to be able to make up the slack if Santa fell short. "I say, Virgil, I hope you will let me play with some of your presents," he said. Virgil assured him that his offer was welcome.

When they rejoined Clarissa in the living room, Tom noticed how sparsely decorated for Christmas the house was. In fact, the only evidence of holiday spirit to be seen besides the poinsettia and the Nativity set was a bowl full of Christmas cards. Otherwise the house fairly drooped for want of Christmas cheer. His poinsettia had brought a dash of color to what would otherwise have been a drab scene.

Clarissa explained the family's Christmas Eve traditions to her guests. Essentially these consisted of dinner and then some caroling around the piano. After Virgil and Horace had gone to bed, the adults would stay up for a while and decorate the Christmas tree. Irene intended to go to midnight Mass. When he heard this, Tom volunteered to accompany her.

Dinner was pleasant. Conversation lingered over comments on country versus city living and the current offerings in the theatre. After dinner they processed into the living room where Irene lit a vigil light by the crèche and Horace placed the Baby Jesus in the manager while everyone sang "Silent Night." Then Joe played the piano while the others stood around and caroled. They soon worked their way through "O Holy Night" and "Good King Wenceslas," Tom taking the part of the king. Virgil and Horace chimed in on "The Drummer Boy" and "Jingle Bells." Clarissa, Tom and Bill entertained the assemblage with a couple of excerpts from "The Messiah." At this point Virgil and Horace started nodding, and soon their elders trundled them off to bed.

Once they had disappeared, the company labored to make a Christmas tree stowed behind a shed appear in the living room, and Tom began to understand why Frossie's husband had greeted them so warmly at the train station a few hours before. At last the tree stood erect and decorated with twinkling lights and an angel on top and a snowy coverlet below. The ladies handed out ornaments to the gentlemen who found suitable boughs on which to hang them. And then the tree was done and gifts for Virgil and Horace artfully placed around its base. Tom and Irene climbed into their boots and coats to drive over to the village church while the others sat around in armchairs and chatted. Cheerily they wished each other a Merry Christmas, and Tom and Irene stepped out into the brisk winter air.

In the car on the drive over to the church Irene was lavish in her praise for the poinsettia. Then she shifted to a more serious topic. "It gets me down that my daughters don't go to church," she said. "When they were children, I took them religiously." She paused and smiled at her choice of language. "When I look back on it, I realize that we didn't have much family prayer – just grace before meals. My husband's opposition discouraged me from undertaking else. I thought they would learn their religion in church, but I guess it was not enough. When they got older, they followed their father's example. That's why I don't have the heart to decorate. I just put up the crib and that's it." Tom felt sorry about the situation, but there was nothing he could do. Irene shifted to a happier topic. She told him about the pastor and what he might expect to see and hear at the Christmas celebration.

At length they arrived, and Tom soon found himself singing "Adeste Fideles" in a pew alongside Irene. The sermon was interesting, with a bit of Scriptural exegesis and an aside from the *Times* Book Review Section thrown in.

They emerged an hour later with a sense of well-being. Irene wanted to go to the ensuing reception in the church hall, and Tom graciously acquiesced. She soon found her friends, and Tom looked around to see if he could spark a conversation in the vicinity. He noticed that couples separated as they entered the hall so men ended up talking to other men and women to other women. Tom thought this over and came to the conclusion that conversational circles were based on interests. Men were discussing sports and business, whereas women were talking about their houses and their children. Tom was beginning to feel like a Christmas orphan in earnest when a dark-haired girl in a long black coat on which a poinsettia corsage floated wandered in. Tom felt a mysterious euphoria come over him the moment he saw her. He could scarce contain himself. He covered the distance between them in giant steps and bent a glowing face down on her. "Can I get you something?" he queried the vision. He did not know what else to say.

"No, actually. I'm just here for conversation," she smiled back.

"Are you from these parts?" Tom asked the dream.

"No, my parents moved here recently. I live in the city."

"So do I. I'm a stranger here too. I just came tonight to keep someone's mother company." He hoped he did not sound too eager.

"I came to celebrate Christmas," she rejoined. "My parents don't go past Santa Claus."

Having established those preliminaries, they commenced a conversation on their respective haunts and adventures in the city. By the time Irene bobbed into sight and signaled she was ready to go, Tom had secured his new acquaintance's name and telephone number. On the way back to the house his hostess chatted about everything that had transpired that evening, but Tom was full of silent joy and not feeling like much of an orphan anymore.

A Verona Interlude

Mystical experience is not an everyday occurrence for most people. In fact, large swaths of the human race manage to live a whole lifetime with little experience of the divine. Some individuals can say they have experienced the Divinity on rare occasions, whereas the saints, if they are not in "the dark night of the soul," claim mystical moments as a frequent occurrence. Nonetheless, an experience of the Creator occurs on a low level to all men of good will. They feel at peace with God, with themselves and with other human beings. They are living in love and have a sense of well-being.

Some have accessed mystical experience by dint of prodigies of prayer, ascetics and works of charity. Others have had group mystical experiences after they have made a prodigious collaborative effort on a spiritual project. For some, it happens when they "fall in love." A few have had this wondrous experience by reason of the prayers of someone who was living on a high spiritual level. Such was the case of Diane Wyrough while she was touring Europe one summer in the company of two girlfriends.

This is the story of her first mystical experience which she recounted many years later when such had become more frequent in her life.

On a lazy afternoon in mid-July Diane, who was between her junior and senior years in college, settled down in her hotel room at the Colomba d'Oro in Verona to read Shakespeare. Her friends Kay and Louise had wanted to go shopping, but Diane had begged off. Somehow, riffling through souvenir shops and clothing stores did not appeal to her that much. They had spent the morning visiting Juliet's house and the sights that were familiar to Shakespeare when he toured Italy during his lost years. Afterwards they had had lunch at a sidewalk café. Now all Diane wanted to do was relax in their hotel room and reread passages from "Romeo and Juliet."

She opened her copy of the play to the balcony scene and read in a lilting voice.

> *But soft, what light through yonder window breaks?*
> *It is the east, and Juliet is the sun.*

Diane sighed. It was so beautiful. She read on silently. Then she came to some of her favorite poetry and read again out loud.

> *She speaks.*
> *O speak again, bright angel, for thou art*
> *As glorious to this night being o'er my head*
> *As is a winged messenger of heaven*
> *Unto the white-upturned wondering eyes*
> *Of mortals that fall back to gaze on him*
> *When he bestrides the lazy-pacing clouds*
> *And sails upon the bosom of the air.*

Suddenly a feeling of weariness came over her. The lines that usually evoked emotion now left her feeling languid. She put the book down and looked out the window. The city of Verona stretched out invitingly before her. She thought perhaps she would do a bit of exploring after all. The old city might have something else to offer besides a setting for a playwright's imagination.

A few minutes later Diane slipped out of the lobby of the Colomba d'Oro and directed her steps toward the center of the city. She thought she would walk around randomly and see what turned up. After an hour of strolling about, she espied a centuries-old church that resembled nothing so much as a graying dowager crumbling around the edges. The prospect of resting her bones for a few moments in the dimly-lit interior appealed to her. She walked into the church and slipped into a pew. Nearby was a statue whose inscription said *"Piero da Verona."* Diane wondered vaguely who he might be. Some saint whom only the people of Verona remembered, she thought.

She knelt for a while in prayer. She had a lot to pray for – her studies, her family and friends, etc. After a while she exited the pew and walked around the church, admiring the stained-glass windows and the statuary. At length she regained the street and then noticed an elderly nun. She was sitting by the door on a folding chair reading a prayerbook and holding a basket in her lap. Diane decided that the nun represented a worthy cause and searched her wallet. When she dropped some euros into the basket, the grandmotherly nun smiled and murmured, *"Grazie. Dio ti benedica."* Diane smiled in return.

As she walked down the street, suddenly a pleasant tingling sensation came over her. She had never felt this way before. She knew, however, that it had to be a mystical experience. The nun must have prayed for me, she thought. She kept walking amid the hustle and bustle of downtown Verona, feeling all the while in a euphoric state. When the sensation finally ended, she glanced at her watch and discovered that the afternoon had slipped away.

She hurried back to the Colomba d'Oro. Louise and Kay were waiting for her in their room. Kay had so much to tell her. "You will never guess what happened. We ran into David Bunting, an old friend from my hometown, and he is sightseeing here in Verona with two friends. They have invited us all to dinner in the old city and then we will see what is available by way of night life. How lucky can you get?"

Diane responded with enthusiasm and joined in the evening's festivities. The following day she kept to their sightseeing schedule as if nothing had happened. She stored up her experience in Verona in her memory and mentioned it to no one.

For a while thereafter whenever she saw an elderly nun sitting with a basket and about her prayers, Diane gave her a charitable contribution. She was disappointed, however, to find that her generosity was not rewarded with another mystical experience. After a number of years had gone by, she happened on Yves Girard's *Blessed Solitude* which explained the gratuitous nature of mystical moments. Then she realized that the purity of intention with which she initially gave to an elderly nun had elicited a mystical experience. When she gave to elderly nuns with the thought that she would be recompensed by another such experience, nothing happened. She came to the conclusion that reciprocity is not the order of the day in the mystical realm. Mystical pleasures, she thought, are an experience of God Who is Love and occur when an individual's motivation is love rather than the calculation of a return on an investment.

Instinct

Society runs along twilight trails in uncharted woods and at any moment something unforeseen may develop. The social ambience is sometimes deflected in its trajectory by natural disaster, untoward bumps in the road, an ethical consideration, and the woods themselves are full of subterfuges and anomalies. A man may easily get lost and not know which way to turn, and it is then that he either consults some inner voice or he relies on instinct, the resort of animals. If instinct is his choice, the environment will cue his actions and he will tend to stay with whatever herd is in his immediate vicinity.

These thoughts and others of a more personal nature were rambling through Rainer Echterling's head as he sat reading an article in the latest issue of *Scientific American* entitled "Instinct in *Homo Sapiens.*" He was ensconced in a comfortable chair behind a desk in the paneled den of his home in Basking Ridge, New Jersey. It was Christmas Eve, and he could see the late afternoon sun glowing orange in the west.

The elderly widower had few callers these days. He had devoted most of his life to managing research projects for the Staub Corporation, mostly at their laboratory in Santa Paula, California. When he acquired the house eons ago, his wife Emma and son Josh had provided an atmosphere of cheer and harmony that had made life worth living and his efforts in the workaday world worthwhile.

Rainer sighed and continued to read. A primitive society that runs on instinct will have utterly different approaches and outcomes from those achieved by a modern society which rises above its natural instincts and reaches for a higher, more humane way of life. In a modern society, love and personality will sublimate the instincts with which Nature has endowed *homo sapiens*. Thus a man acting according to the sublimated mating instinct will interface with women in a courteous and friendly way.

Sitting ensconced behind an oak desk in the tastefully furnished den, Rainer found that everything reminded him of Emma. The pale blue patterned sofa and matching armchairs and white carpeting all bespoke her classical tastes. The colorful bookjackets alternating on the wall-to-wall bookshelves displayed her keen interest in English literature.

Rainer had been proud of his wife. Emma had her Ph.D. in English literature from Yale University and had taught at Seton Hall University for many years. Since her dissertation on Eudora Welty had been published, she was a recognized authority on short American fiction. That was the course she taught to English majors – Short American Fiction. Rainer was happy that she had carved out a niche for herself in academia. Not everyone could boast of a wife who was a college professor. And that was why he had to listen to her arguments for staying in Basking Ridge when Staub transferred him to its research facility in Santa Paula. He remembered well how tenaciously she had argued against moving to California. She was cogent, passionate and utterly intransigent. He had realized early on that there was no persuading her to another point of view. He had to admit that the market for English professors was saturated. Even having published a monograph, Emma would probably not be able to find a position comparable to the one she had at Seton Hall. So he had acquiesced to living weekdays in Santa Paula and weekends in Basking Ridge. It was a long commute, but being with Emma on Saturdays and Sundays made it all worthwhile. In the evenings they usually went to plays, readings and lectures on campus or to a faculty party so he felt great continuity in his social circle. On Sunday mornings they went to church, and there again Rainer had many acquaintances with whom to chat during the coffee hour after Mass. What seemed awkward initially had thus become part of his accepted routine. He had lived uncomplaining on both coasts for upwards of thirty years.

It had begun to snow outside, and Rainer went to the window to look out. He gauged the accumulation as still negligible, not enough to require shoveling. He hoped this would not stop Constance from picking him up for midnight Mass. She had promised to do so, but a blizzard would definitely cancel that good intention. Constance was a single woman in her forties who was given to good works such as looking in on the elderly. Rainer was happy to be the recipient of her charity. She also took him grocery shopping on Saturday mornings, at which time he was able to supply all his needs. Thus Constance was the *sine qua non* of his independent existence, and Rainer was careful to reciprocate by inviting her to dinner at various restaurants in the vicinity. He suspected that Constance was no cook and was happy to be rescued from an existence based on delicatessen sandwiches.

Otherwise he was fairly housebound. He had lost his ability to drive shortly after Emma's demise and was able now to manage only short walks in the neighborhood.

In winter the biting wind drove him indoors and walking around the house provided his only exercise aside from the short jaunts with Constance.

He had so looked forward to retirement. He had thought it would be a welcome respite from the continental commute and he would have time to dip into intellectual areas that had been pre-empted by his focus on work. For a while the promise which retirement had held seemed to be fulfilled. He had plunged with abandon into the classics of ancient Greece and Rome and then waded through the biographies and histories that were making the bestseller lists. He had been reading widely in these areas when the shock of Emma's unexpected death unnerved him. He had walked into her bedroom one afternoon to find her lying on the bed as cold as a sphinx. She did not respond to his voice, and he had wept.

Emma had been his life, and now that life unraveled. A few months after her death he lost his ability to drive and with it a lot of his interest in the outside world. Occasionally he picked up a biography now, but he found it difficult to get absorbed in a life so different from his own.

At the wake and funeral Josh had barely spoken to him. At the time Rainer had attributed his son's silence to grief. When after the funeral Josh made no attempt to contact him, he had to re-examine this assumption. He recollected also that Emma had left all the assets she had inherited from her parents to Josh. Thus he and his son had not even met for business reasons.

Boarding school had become Josh's destiny at age ten because Emma wanted him to have the best possible education. They saw him at Thanksgiving and Christmas and on a few other holidays. In the summer he went away to camp, again to have the most opportunities. Rainer had to admit that his son had grown up largely without him. Still, Emma had insisted that he was receiving the best possible education, and when he was accepted at Harvard, her view seemed to be vindicated. Josh had continued on for the Ph.D. and had become an assistant professor at Columbia University. He had subsequently married and had bought a house in South Orange, an easy commute to the city. He regularly dropped over for Sunday dinner with his wife and children so Rainer felt no sense of discontinuity. Now that Emma was gone, however, these visits came to an abrupt end. It was as if Josh had dropped off the planet. Rainer was forced to revisit his relationship with his son.

The snow was tapering off. It looked like midnight Mass would be possible after all. Rainer was glad. It would be a shame not to go to church on Christmas Day. The choir would be inspired. They might even sing "Gesù Bambino," his favorite.

He stared at the periodical open on his desk and returned to his ruminations. He had little company these days except for his thoughts so he reviewed the question of Josh or, rather, the question of non-Josh. Why did he not come or call? Did he love only his mother but not his father? Had boarding school lessened his feelings for his father? Rainer had to conclude in the affirmative. But Josh evidently still had a feeling for his mother who had made the boarding school and summer camp decisions. What was the difference between Emma and him? Was it specific to them, or was it the difference between a mother and a father? Rainer had been carrying this question around in his head for a couple of weeks when he came across the article in *Scientific American*. As he looked down at it now lying on his desk, the words "maternal instinct" fairly jumped out at him. He picked up the magazine again and read further. "A child," the article claimed, "has an instinctive feeling for its mother even if she is not particularly warm and loving." Rainer was electrified. This, he felt, was the answer. "On the other hand," the article continued, "a child and its father share no comparable instinctive feelings for each other." Rainer sat bolt upright. He thought he had found the answer to his question. Josh felt an instinctive pull toward his mother even though she had sent him to boarding school and summer camp, whereas there was no instinct drawing him to his father. Rainer had to conclude that Josh's deference to Emma was based on instinct and not on love. Since he did not love his parents, he had no feeling whatsoever for his father. If Emma did not love her son but merely acted according to maternal instinct, Rainer then had to examine the question of whether or not she had loved him.

This was a painful experience. Rainer did not know why he should drudge through it on Christmas Eve. His eyes wandered to the window and drank in a neighbor's twinkling Christmas lights that lit up the inky night. He thought he would prepare dinner and get ready for Constance.

She came at eleven o'clock because she wanted to attend the choir concert that preceded midnight Mass. She left him off at the church entrance and, while he found seats, went to park the car. They settled in for the concert in the third pew. The choir warbled through "O Holy Night" and "Gesù Bambino." Midnight Mass began, and Rainer concentrated on what was being said.

Afterwards Constance drove him home, and Rainer invited her in for some cider and cookies and presented her with a couple of books he had purchased over the Internet. She was leaving in the morning to visit her brother and his family in Maryland so Rainer knew he would not see her again until Saturday morning when she would take him grocery shopping.

On Christmas Day Rainer was up as usual with the dawn. He had nowhere to go, nothing to do, and no one he was expecting. Josh had never called him even on Christmas so he was not anticipating anything from that direction. The first few months after Emma's death he had tried phoning Josh, but he was either out or he was too busy to come over. After that he had left it up to his son to initiate a meeting, but he had waited in vain. This had gone on for several years, and Rainer had given up hope.

And so on Christmas morning he was truly alone. He put on "The Messiah" and listened for a while. The afternoon came and the sunlight glistened on the snow outside. It was a fairyland, but Rainer felt he might as well be living in a desert. "O dear God!" he cried out suddenly. "Doesn't he know that I love him? Doesn't he care?" Just at that moment a car swung into the driveway. A young woman jumped out and walked briskly to the door.

"Who can it be?" Rainer wondered. The doorbell rang and he shuffled to the door to answer it.

"Grandpa!" exclaimed a cheery young face surrounded by luscious black curls and topped by a white fur hat.

"Brianna, is that you? I haven't seen you in so long I didn't recognize you!" he gasped.

She kissed him on the cheek and said, "Well, aren't you going to invite me in?"

"Yes, yes, of course. I am just so surprised. Come in! Come in!"

She swept into the living room and looked around, her eyes wide open with wonder.

"It is just as I remember it. Everything is just where Grandma left it. You haven't changed a thing."

"No, I haven't," he admitted. "I am not much of a decorator." He had always maintained careful boundaries between what he would and would not do around the house. Taking an interest in interior design had always seemed to be Emma's province, and he left it to her even now.

"But I miss the crèche! Where is the crèche?" Rainer had to confess it was in the basement. Then nothing would do but she had to descend the steps to the nether regions of the house to fetch it. As she lovingly took out the porcelain figures one by one and assigned them a place in a stable made of log chips on the coffee table in the living room, Brianna filled him in on what she had been doing in the dramatic society in college and how much she enjoyed a particular course that encompassed Jonathan Swift and the eminent Mr. Johnson himself. Along the way she mentioned that she had joined a prayer group that had opened up whole new vistas of spiritual insight for her. Rainer was amazed. No one in the family had ever been interested in religion except in the most conventional way. Sunday church had represented a cultural heritage to Emma, and he marveled that Brianna seemed to take it so to heart.

When Brianna left him a couple of hours later, she promised to return the following day and drive him around town to see the Christmas lights. Rainer was content. He thought he would throw out the *Scientific American* he found lying on the floor of the den.

La Gourmande

Jamie Cornwall (or J.C. as she was known to her acquaintances) watched sprawling suburban homes slowly yield to drab blocks of shoebox houses snuggled up against one another as her train slogged along through the Jersey hinterland on its way to the great metropolis. As she looked out the window, she barely noticed the brilliant sunset out to the west lighting up the winter landscape that shifted between frozen brown tundra and the snowy remnants of last weekend's blizzard. J.C. was not the romantic sort. For her, a sunset was a reflection on cloud particles, not a dreamy mirror of the appetites of earth encountering the revelations of the heavens. So it had once been described to her by one Timothy O'Donnell, a young man she had met on her visits to the coral reefs in Yucatan. J.C. had stared at him in disbelief and was forming the distinct impression in her mind that he was daft when he smiled and joked her out of it. Yes, she had been reared in the rarified realm of science and did not have a romantic bone in her body. That was why she was puzzled when every spring she felt some vague longing, some indefinable passion that did not normally course in her veins. It had happened to her again this spring, and this time she had resolved to do something about it. That was why she was en route to a rendezvous with a stranger negotiated over the Internet.

At the ripe old age of 27, with a Ph.D. in Marine Biology, J.C. was at that stage in her life when she thought wedding bells should be ringing. While she had been drudging away at nailing down a Ph.D. and securing a foothold in the job market, the biological clock had been ticking and now she felt she had to take some action.

J.C. was an only child whose father, a surgeon, had encouraged her to follow in his footsteps. Her mother, a concert pianist, played Chopin and Liszt on the baby grand piano in the living room so J.C. came naturally by the idea that she, too, should acquire some area of expertise. In this endeavor she had single-mindedly pursued the Ph.D. in the classrooms and laboratories of a certain eminent university in Cambridge, Massachusetts. Graduate school had been an exciting time although she would admit to a few doldrums in the dissertation writing stage. Still, she had persevered and had finished the race. She had graduated with a doctorate at age 26, and her thesis was abstracted in the *Journal of Marine Biology*.

At the time she entered the job market, however, it was crammed full of Ph.D.'s looking for professional employment. The only offer she had was an assistant professorship in Boulder, Colorado. She thought Marine Biology might have more going on in the environs of New York City so she had accepted a position as an adjunct professor in the Evening Division at Ramapo College of New Jersey with the thought that she would live with her parents and see what research opportunities she could find. And at the very least she would be a lot nearer the ocean than the Boulder location afforded

At Ramapo she was teaching biology in the evenings and on Saturdays to freshmen who were taking it as a required course. She had hopes, however, of working her way up the ladder from this obscure status. She expected to continue her research on newly discovered marine species and to gain recognition by publishing her findings. Eventually she might win tenure at some prestigious university and then be in a good position for the rest of her life.

J.C. remembered her graduation well. Her father had beamed proudly at her. Her mother, too, had seemed happy that her daughter had finally attained her dream. They knew that Ramapo College's Evening Division lay in her immediate future, but they also thought that, with a bit of work, this situation would change.

Her parents lived in Upper Saddle River, a community which was not too far from the college. As she was not exactly financially above the salt as an adjunct professor, living with her parents seemed the obvious thing to do. Since they were quiet, gentle folk, living with them represented an advantage with no corresponding disadvantages attached.

Occasionally J.C. discussed her research and her classes with her father. He loved hearing about her efforts to make the classes interesting to her students and how she tried to generate classroom discussion. Sometimes he said she was turning business majors into biologists. They both laughed at that.

Her mother left them alone for their biology conversations, as she termed them. She did, however, have an opinion on another topic. One day J.C. was listening to her mother playing the Moonlight Sonata when suddenly her parent looked at her and remarked, "It is time you were getting married, dear. Otherwise how will we have grandchildren running under foot?"

J.C. blurted out, "I know, I know. I just haven't found the right man yet."

Her mother's fingers came to a halt as she pondered this response. Then she returned to the attack.

"Have you tried the Internet? Maybe you can find someone through a dating service."

"That's a thought," J.C. glumly admitted.

Her mother pressed her advantage. "You can list all the attributes you are looking for in a man and see what the computer comes up with."

It sounded reasonable, and J.C. knew she had had little luck with conventional approaches. The young men she met in biology laboratories were intent on their careers and interacted with her warily, steering the conversation away from personal matters. Evidently they preferred not to think of her as a female. As for men outside her field, she simply did not meet them. She disliked discotheques with their loud music and had no girlfriends who were interested in fixing her up with a date. She had ended up postponing thinking about marriage until after she had obtained her Ph.D.

Now, of course, the time had arrived. She had been teaching in the Ramapo College Evening Division for almost two semesters and was beginning to feel secure in her position. After all, how could the administration find someone who was willing to work for less? J.C. sighed. Yes, she felt secure in her position.

The following day in an idle moment she looked for matchmaking services on the Internet. She chose Dating Singles and filled in all the relevant information. She did not want to forestall any prospective interest so she listed herself as a biology teacher who had a Master's degree in the field. That was technically correct although it was obviously not the whole truth.

She was listed on the Dating Singles website a few days later and was curiously eager to see what sort of interest her profile would elicit. A week went by. Then she had an e-mail from a petroleum engineer on the North Slope of Alaska. He was 30, had an engineering degree from Texas A&M and was interested in football, movies and jazz. J.C. found his geography disconcerting and supposed that probably they did not have much in common.

A day later she heard from a diplomat stationed in Osaka. He was 25 years old and had a Master's degree in International Relations from Georgetown University. He listed his interests as history, foreign languages and classical music. His profile cast a more romantic penumbra than had the credentials of the petroleum engineer, but J.C. felt fairly certain she did not want to live abroad on a permanent basis.

The third hit was closer to home. John Aubuisson was a manager, age 37, who lived in Rye, New York and had a bachelor's degree in Business Administration from New York University. He was also a widower with three children, ages ten, seven and three. J.C. had to admire him for being honest and decided to give him a chance.

He replied immediately to her e-mail.

"Hi, Jamie! You sound like a nice person. Your experience of having hits from the other end of the world is probably not an uncommon one. I guess that makes me singular, doesn't it? Someone who practically lives in the neighborhood.

"You say you live with your parents. Well, we have something in common right off the bat. My mother lives with me and takes care of the children. Her husband and my wife having gone to their eternal rewards, we thought this was the best of all possible arrangements.

"Tell me, how do you keep the gremlins under control? I refer to your students. I have heard that students nowadays are terrible monsters. Or perhaps you have discovered some secret for keeping them from perpetrating the usual hyperactivity in your classroom.

"I ask out of idle curiosity. You don't have to answer.

"My own children are as good as gold. I think they take after me."

He signed his e-mail "Yours, John."

J.C. considered this to be a fairly good effort in e-mail correspondence. He is at ease with strangers, she thought. He surmises that I am teaching high school biology. I won't disabuse him of that notion. I don't want to overwhelm him with my academic credentials before we have even met. Besides, my job has nothing to do with my personal life. She decided to reply in the same lighthearted vein.

"None of my students is a 'gremlin.' The worst they might do is cut class. This can be very serious because then they will have missed something important so I try to make my classes so interesting that they will want to be there. It is easy to make biology interesting. It is, after all, the story of life." She signed off "Yours, J.C." and sent it.

The following day a reply showed up on her screen.

"Are you J.C. or Jamie? Shall I sign myself J.A.? What is the protocol here?

"Although we do not live on opposite sides of the world from each other, we do inhabit different neighborhoods. Perhaps we could settle on an intermediate location and meet there. Are you game?" He signed it "John or J.A."

Of course, she was dying to see what he looked like. She supposed he was equally curious about her and thought he would not be disappointed. She decided to go ahead.

"I answer to either Jamie or J.C. I am game to meet so long as it is not too far out of the way. Where do you suggest?"

He proposed meeting at *La Gourmande*, a French restaurant in midtown Manhattan, that Saturday night.

And so she was on a train easing into Penn Station late Saturday afternoon wondering what to expect.

La Gourmande turned out to be a posh French restaurant with an intimate, dimly-lit interior. Red votive lights twinkled on square tables placed here and there, and an occasional ballet dancer pirouetted or preened in Impressionist paintings hung on ruddy walls that receded into the darkness. The *maître de* approached J.C. and inquired if she had a reservation. When she used Mr. Aubuisson's name, he raised his eyebrows slightly, then smiled and showed her to a table half hidden in a corner behind an exotic plant. The *sommelier* appeared with a wine list, but she declined to order before her host arrived. Just as the *sommelier* was departing, a youngish man with auburn hair and a twinkle in his blue eyes appeared and motioned him to remain. The youngish man smiled broadly at J.C. and introduced himself as John Aubuisson. With an air of authority he said, "Jamie, we must order something. It is the custom of the house. What will you have?"

J.C. searched her limited knowledge of French *apéritifs* and decided to order a daiquiri. Her new acquaintance smiled and requested a Perrier.

"Did you have any trouble finding the place?" he inquired.

"No, your directions were quite explicit."

"Did you come by taxi?"

"No, by subway. I like the subway. Taxis are so expensive."

"You're thrifty, I see." Then, lest he give the impression that he was assessing her, he changed the subject slightly. "A lot of people arrive here on foot. They just descend from their *pied-à-terres* in the neighborhood and walk over.

The *sommelier* returned and meticulously placed their drinks in the positions dictated by etiquette. When her host thanked him appreciatively, the man came briefly to attention and then disappeared.

"Jacques was in the military," her host observed casually. "He likes to make his presentations with a flourish." Then he looked at her more earnestly. "Jamie, let's drink to us and to the Internet which has brought us to this happy ambience."

She felt she could drink to that. It was a light comment, and she was feeling mellow.

A few minutes later a waiter approached and they ordered. J.C. could tell that the waiter was quite familiar with John Aubuisson. Perhaps he came here often.

"Do you come here often?" she asked politely.

"Too often," he replied. "I have to come here. It's my business. I mean, I am the manager and co-owner of the place. I come here every day except Monday. My partner comes on Mondays and goes over the books." J.C. thought she detected a slight wince flit over his features on the last comment.

That solved one mystery. He had said on the Internet that he was a manager. Now she knew of what.

They proceeded slowly and conversationally through dinner. He traveled sometimes to France where he had relatives. He was bilingual. J.C. admired that. She had studied Greek, Latin, French and German and had acquired a smattering of Spanish, but she had never attained fluency in any language other than English.

Altogether it was a pleasant evening. Around nine o'clock he said he would have to let her find her way home; he would be staying at the restaurant until midnight at least and in any case her neighborhood was a bit out of the way for someone from Rye. He invited her to come again on the following Saturday.

This became a pattern over the next few weekends. J.C. found herself increasingly looking forward to her Saturday night dates at *La Gourmande*. She caught herself daydreaming at odd moments, thinking about John and analyzing his comments. John was low-key, she decided, but she could sense that he was a compassionate soul. Sometimes she thought she saw a love light in his eyes. She wondered if it was for her or if he looked at everyone that way. Occasionally he said something funny, especially when he talked about his children. He also shared with her his philosophy of management with respect to *La Gourmande*. He told her they sent leftovers to a soup kitchen run by a church in the neighborhood. Another time he mentioned that he paid his staff a little above the market rate so they tended to stay for a long time. At Christmas he gave the staff a party at *El Quijote* where there was a classical guitarist and a flamenco dancer.

    She noticed that sometimes he lingered thoughtfully as he helped her slip into her coat, but he never tried to touch her unnecessarily or to kiss her even on the cheek. J.C. pondered this. Of course, the coatcheck girl was standing nearby and patrons were walking past, circumstances that might explain his reserve, but J.C. thought it was more than that.

    John never spoke of his late wife, but in response to a question he had divulged her name, Angela, and the fact that she was indeed an angel, then and now. He had not wanted to talk more about her and so J.C. had not pressed the matter. Similarly, she had resolved never to mention marine biology lest she scare him off. In effect, she was content to let him take the conversational lead.

    He asked about her parents early on. J.C. gave him a quick sketch of their domestic bliss, and he seemed satisfied with this.

    As the flowered panoply of March and April progressed in the suburbs, J.C. found herself responding emotionally and daydreaming at odd hours about her Saturday night beau. She wondered about what he was thinking and whether he was falling in love with her, although she was not actually sure what falling in love meant. Perhaps it meant thinking about someone a lot or smiling to oneself for no particular reason.

Her mother had guessed immediately that her daughter was dating someone on Saturday nights. J.C. told her she was going to Manhattan, and they left it at that. On the third such tryst her mother suggested that she borrow some of her jewelry so J.C. selected some diamond earrings for the occasion. John was impressed. "So you like diamonds, Jamie?" She nodded, unsure if she should tell him their provenance. He seemed about to say something more, but then he stopped himself. Jamie smiled and sparkled. He watched her but kept his own counsel.

When she finally checked the Dating Singles website again, she found she had a message that was a few days old. It was from a computer analyst in Brooklyn who visited discotheques in his spare time. She decided not to reply. She thought John, too, was no longer interested in Dating Singles. At least he never mentioned it.

This kind of dating pattern had been going on for a couple of months when one Saturday when she arrived at the restaurant for their usual rendezvous, she found two small faces sitting one on either side of John at the table. The two faces belonged to Amy, age seven, and Rémi, age three. Gabrielle, John's oldest, was singing in a glee club concert at St. Walburga's and John's mother had gone to represent the family. Amy turned out to be a precocious little girl who nonetheless knew when to keep quiet, and Rémi was adept at following her lead. Dinner proceeded rather agreeably although Amy avowed a distinct preference for hamburgers over French cuisine. By about the time they were finishing their entrées, she proved her point by regurgitating her *coq au vin*. J.C. was aghast. How horrid, she thought. John mopped his daughter's dress with a napkin and asked Jamie to take the girl to the restroom where she puked some more and cried. J.C. was nonplussed. She had never felt the lack of a course in Early Childhood before. At length Amy felt she was done and they returned to the table in embarrassed silence. At this point Rémi chimed in that he had to go to the toilet so his father hustled him off to the men's room. J.C. knew that if they were married, this task would have fallen to her. Suddenly an image of dirty baby diapers flashed before her eyes. When John and Rémi returned, it was obvious that the children had had enough excitement for one evening so the waiter whisked them off to a room furnished with a couple of beds.

Seeing her surprised look John explained, "We keep a couple of beds ready in case we have to stay overnight. Sometimes there are weather emergencies or power outages."

Then he invited her again for the following Saturday. This time she had to demur, however. It was going to be her father's birthday, and she had to help her parents celebrate. John understood and said, "Well, then, how about Friday?" She agreed and they left it at that.

The following Friday J.C. found herself once again on the train slogging through suburbia on the way to New York and *La Gourmande*. During the week she had been preoccupied with making arrangements for a trip that summer to the Great Barrier Reef on a work-study program so the episode with the children had dimmed in her memory. Now, however, she had time to think. What was she getting herself into? What if his mother should be unable to continue caring for the children? Would she hire a nanny? She had read an article once about the negative consequences of that policy. Then, too, Gabrielle, Amy and Rémi might be just the start of their family. How many children did she want to have? These and other questions were troubling her when she walked through the doors of *La Gourmande*. John was waiting for her as usual, welcoming her with a winning smile.

"You're a real trooper, Jamie," he chuckled. "I guess after dissecting all those frogs, nothing my children can do would upset you." She smiled and turned her attention to the menu. On Fridays she abstained from meat so she asked for a vegetarian dish. John was feeling expansive and ordered lobster. Then he chatted on about the market for French wine, and J.C. basked in his attention and engaging manners.

When their entrées arrived, John attacked his lobster with gusto. J.C. thought of the hours she had spent in the laboratory dissecting the crustacean's cousins and the odor of formaldehyde came sensibly to her nostrils. She tried to concentrate on what her host was saying about sauternes, but that only added to the culinary mess.

Then suddenly out of the blue he changed the subject. "By the way," he said, "what do you think of Rebecca Freitag being appointed to head up the space effort?" Not waiting for a response, he added, "I don't care what she is, a professor at M.I.T. or the village idiot. We shouldn't have a woman managing anything with that kind of risk level. There must be plenty of men around who are qualified for the position. Why are they selecting her?"

J.C. answered tentatively. "Because she has been successful in her previous assignments?"

"I don't care if she has been successful or not. Men are better than women in high-risk situations and ought to manage anything of that nature. Let her manage something that isn't so risky or do lab research or teach if that is her thing."

"Do you think all women should stay in the laboratory or the classroom?" she bristled.

"No, of course not, but I don't think women should be managing anything where people's lives are on the line and so much can go wrong." Giving Jamie a fierce look, he said, "And what is more, I don't cotton to all these female Ph.D.'s and college professors."

J.C. was getting hot under the collar. "I am a female Ph.D. and college professor," she exclaimed. He gazed at her in shock. "Yes," she averred, "I teach biology at Ramapo College of New Jersey." She declined to enlighten him on her status as an adjunct professor teaching freshman biology in the Evening Division.

He stared at her, his mouth gaping. When he finally recovered his senses, he gasped, "You are a Ph.D. and a college professor? What have I lucked into?"

J.C. realized she had probably damaged their relationship irretrievably and thought she had better change the subject. After all, she was his guest. "Tell me, how do you select the sauternes?" she managed.

"The magazines write them up so we know the best years and vintners. They pretty much stay the same year after year," he replied mechanically. Then he said, "Jamie, don't you think it was a bit unethical for you to list yourself as simply an M.A. and a biology teacher, thereby leading me to think that you were a high school teacher?"

"But I thought I might turn men off if they knew the truth."

"Jamie, what do you want in life?"

"I, I don't know. Everything, I suppose."

"You can't have everything. Life isn't like that. We all have to specialize. One thing militates against another. Andrew Carnegie said, 'Put all your eggs in one basket and then watch that basket.'" He paused, reflecting on the sense behind this *bon mot*. Then he continued, "What kind of person are you, Jamie? Are you a career woman or would you like to get married and have children? I think these are two different lives. No one can handle both well."

"But your mother ..."

"My mother wants to move to Florida. She says the winters here are too much for her old bones."

"Oh!..."

Donnybrook

South of the centre of Dublin lies an old district called Donnybrook where in the days of King John a fair was held that became the scene of drunken brawls. On market days the yeomen from the surrounding countryside descended on the fair grounds ad, with a couple of pints of good ale releasing their inhibitions, set to and worked out their aggressions on their fellowmen. As there was no arbiter, the Donnybrook brawl continued into the night until all the participants were laid low. The local constabulary was reluctant to intervene, thinking it would take an army to restore the peace and not wanting to throw a feather into the jaws of a maelstrom. As a consequence, the term Donnybrook became an eponym for rough and rowdy free-for-alls. The fair was finally banned by the authorities in 1855, and in modern times the neighborhood has taken on a genteel air. A totally different mix of inhabitants enjoying the benefits of education and affluence has made Donnybrook a prime residential area in Dublin. The typical townsman is a person of distinction in his field, whether as a writer of novels, of laws or of scholarly tomes.

Thus the reputation of Donnybrook teeters between the drunken brawls of past centuries and the urbanity and gentility of modern times.

Not a few devils still lurk in the neighborhood, however. From time to time they emerge when family members clobber one another or young bullies set upon a passing acquaintance. In support of notions of societal evolution, modern sessions of atavistic violence are usually confined to verbal sallies, and are not out and out physical assaults. Nonetheless, collapsed personalities still haunt the streets and darker nooks of Donnybrook, throwing an occasional fright into its less muscly inhabitants. The menace lingers on, and more civilized souls are sometimes hard put to ensure the preservation of the amenities.

I

A stylishly-dressed brunette in her mid-forties, Laurentia Vann had lived in Donnybrook her entire married life, only occasionally leaving the comfortable confines of Ireland to travel to Britain or the Continent. It was with some trepidation one day in late February, therefore, that she boarded a flight heading in the general direction of Australia. After a short hop to Frankfurt, she set out on the long jaunt to the southern hemisphere. She had brought along a couple of historical novels to read on the plane and so whiled away the lengthy flight soaking up the atmosphere of Old Vienna and Weimar in its heyday.

When the plane finally circled Sydney Harbor and approached for a landing, Laurentia thought she had never before seen such a paradise. The Opera House fluttered on the edge of the bay; the blue water of the ocean indented the encrustations of men. At a time when Ireland was laboring under its version of winter, Sydney was emerging from its annual brush with the tropics. Laurentia waltzed through customs daydreaming about what might be awaiting her in this southern clime. Professor Sturmi Ziesel, a tall, handsome Austrian in his fifties, was standing by the exit. He had said he would be sporting a Tirolean hat, and she had promised to wear a navy blue suit with a white scarf so they had no trouble identifying each other. Sturmi, as he preferred to be called, had been assigned to shepherd her around for the first few days and to secure her well-being generally. He took her to the apartment she was subletting from a professor on sabbatical and helped her get settled. That evening he called for her and took her to dinner at the *Heidelberg* where he proceeded to confide his thoughts about the German Romantic movement in general and the European Studies Program in particular. It was all very charming and Laurentia thought she might enjoy her exile after all.

  The following morning the courtly Austrian walked her over to the university which was only a short distance away. He escorted her to a cafeteria on campus where they ordered breakfast. Over ham and eggs he gave her a general orientation to campus life and told her what she could expect as the semester wore on. They then walked around and visited the Great Hall with its stained-glass windows depicting the giants of intellectual history. Laurentia was thrilled. At the European Studies Program office Sturmi introduced her to the director and staff. He also showed her the office she would be sharing with Monique Mirouze, a professor of French literature. Together they found the lecture halls where she would be teaching. Over lunch he regaled her with an account of a comic moment that had occurred backstage during a performance of Goethe's "Faust" in the previous semester. Laurentia felt happy to be part of such a cosmopolitan setting. Then her escort excused himself and left her to wander about the campus on her own, lost in pleasant daydreams with respect to the coming semester.

A couple of days later classes began. That morning Laurentia felt as if she had awakened into a nightmare. Perhaps the excitement of her new surroundings had faded and the uncertainty of beginning classes in a new ambience had darkened her mood, but for some reason all her thoughts were back in Donnybrook. With some misgivings she slipped out of the apartment and started walking toward the university.

Laurentia had come to the University of Sydney on loan from University College Dublin for one semester to teach a course on the European Literary Heritage and one on the Romantic Movement. Her department chairman in Dublin had asked her to take on this assignment at the last minute because Professor Sheehan had suddenly taken ill and was unable to teach as he had planned. The maintenance of friendly relations with the University of Sydney was important to University College Dublin. Consequently, Dr. O'Leary hinted that the Australian assignment was a prerequisite for Laurentia's continuance in his department. Under these circumstances Laurentia had acquiesced. As she walked toward the campus on the first day of classes, however, she found herself worrying about the husband she had left behind. That morning she was not thinking about the lecture she would shortly be presenting on the European Literary Heritage but rather about her marriage.

Twenty-three years ago she had first spoken to Bennet Vann. It was a Saturday evening during a concert intermission at National Concert Hall in Dublin. As a Trinity College undergraduate majoring in Romance languages, she had attended his class on Enlightenment Progressives, but she had never dared to approach him. Tall and auburn-haired, Bennet presided somewhat forbiddingly at the podium. He lambasted critics and satirized opponents. Those he disagreed with came in for a full measure of scorn. Not wishing to be so skewered, Laurentia had steered a wide berth of him.

Bennet was an American by birth and had preceded her into the world by about ten years. His publications had attracted attention in the Old World, and so he had been invited to assume a professorship at Trinity College, that bastion of Enlightenment scholarship. As Laurentia would never have presumed to speak to so exalted a personage when she was an undergraduate, she did not feel much more at ease when she was teaching French at Our Lady of Mercy College in Beaumont.

He had begun the conversation. Their friends had dispersed, and he had turned to her and asked how she liked the Beethoven violin concerto. One comment led to another (he acknowledged that he remembered her from his class), and by the time their friends were returning, he was asking for her telephone number. This had led to other concerts and to plays. She was impressed by his manners and his joshing social banter. She looked forward to their evenings out and was ready to say yes when he popped the big question.

At that point she introduced him to her Aunt Melanie, a maiden lady who taught a course in English Literature from Beowulf to the Romantics at the University of Ireland, Maynooth. Laurentia's father had become a widower relatively early in life. Highly placed in the bureaucracy of the European Union in Brussels, he had experienced no difficulty in locating a second wife. Aurélie was a French heiress who, once her new husband was secured, voiced her reluctance to mother the child of another woman. The care of Laurentia, therefore, devolved upon her Aunt Melanie, and the girl moved from Brussels to Maynooth. As her aunt was a kindly soul, Laurentia believed she inhabited the best of all possible worlds except for the rarity of her father's visits and the lack of siblings. In time she came to have two half-siblings, Jean and

Philippe, and made their acquaintance in passing when they came to summer with Aunt Melanie just as she was exiting to attend a language institute in France or Spain. She vowed that one day she would have a big family in order to make up for this lacuna in her childhood.

Aunt Melanie was cordial to Bennet when they met. Afterwards she wondered privately to Laurentia if marrying an agnostic was a good idea. As Laurentia had already made up her mind with regard to the marriage, she did not trouble herself on this score.

The wedding had gone off like clockwork. Her father had appeared from Brussels to give away the bride, and the wedding reception was attended by a complement of their closest friends and associates. Bennet had no family in Ireland so, of course, none of his relatives was present. His parents were dead, he explained, and now only one sister kept in sporadic touch with him. When Laurentia asked him how many siblings he had, he lapsed into a stony silence. She wondered at this but did not pursue the topic.

Laurentia sighed as she negotiated the sidewalks of Sydney in the proximity of the university. She failed to notice the beckoning shop windows and the exotic restaurants she was passing. As she paused at an intersection, some students were laughing around her. She wondered what was so funny.

Bennet had acquired a home in upscale Donnybrook, and they had settled into married life. Soon after the honeymoon Laurentia discovered that it was now up to her to provide for the conversation. The heady days of courtship were over, and her husband had devolved into a taciturn, mechanical version of his former self. When Laurentia mentioned this to Aunt Melanie, her aunt replied that this condition was not uncommon among agnostics. She advised Laurentia to approach her spouse with jokes and humorous anecdotes to keep him in an affable mood.

Her aunt also thought that if Laurentia invited friends to share their repasts, this might keep Bennet in a happy state of mind. Aunt Melanie issued the newlyweds an open invitation for Sunday dinners in Maynooth. In this way they kept in close touch with her. They also gravitated to Aunt Melanie's for Christmas and other holidays. Maynooth became an oasis of peace in their married life.

Armed with Aunt Melanie's advice, Laurentia set about creating an interesting social life for the two of them. She befriended Vincent O'Malley, a professor emeritus of Modern European History who resided in the neighborhood, and invited him to dinner. Bennet was pleased. She issued a dinner invitation to the novelist Aidan McNabb and his wife Barbara whom she had come to know at St. Mary's Church on Haddington Road. Bennet enjoyed this encounter as well. Then she ventured to invite Father John O'Connor, one of the priests at St. Mary's. Father O'Connor was full of the Patristics lectures being delivered at the weekly papal general audiences in St. Peter's Square and batted these ideas around with Bennet. Her husband decided to accompany Laurentia to the 10:00 a.m. Mass on Sunday mornings so he could gather ammunition from the good priest's sermons for use in future dinner debates.

Thinking to make her conversation more interesting to her husband, Laurentia decided to go for her doctorate in Comparative Literature at University College Dublin. She also began attending Friday evening lectures at the Avila Retreat Centre in Donnybrook. After a time Bennet tagged along and found, to his surprise, that the lectures on St. John of the Cross and other mystics titillated his sense of the beyond. After the lectures there was a social hour during which they made the acquaintance of Father Patrick Flannery, a professor of Spirituality at the seminary, and other clerics and lay luminaries who lived in the vicinity.

And then Baby Stephen had come along. He was a good child. Laurentia carried him to her classes when he was still quite young and dropped him off at school as he got older. She had left him alone with Bennet on one or two occasions while she went shopping and had returned to find the little fellow in tears. After that she took him with her whenever she left the house.

Every once in a while Bennet received a mysterious envelope from America. It came from St. George, Utah, and Laurentia assumed it was from his sister. He never discussed it, never opened it in her presence, and never discarded it in their house. Once she asked how his sister was, but he did not reply. She wondered at this but did not broach the matter again.

When Laurentia obtained her doctorate, the department chairman asked her to teach a course in Modern European Literature. Now, in some small way, she had attained Bennet's status. In this position it seemed only natural to invite visiting lecturers to her home for dinner before they gave their talks. This provided Bennet with a chance to exchange ideas with eminent authors close to his field.

When Stephen got older, they entrusted his education to Belvedere College. At school functions they encountered his Latin teacher, Father Andrew Delaney. Thereafter, whenever Stephen had to be at school in the evening, they asked Father Delaney out to dinner. Their usual haunt for these outings was the *Roman Forum*, an Italian restaurant redolent of ruins and Latin sayings. There Bennet and the classics scholar would joust over the landscape of Western civilization while Laurentia listened to their thrusts and parries with a secret smile.

She remembered in particular one exchange when Father Delaney very earnestly suggested that the civilization of ancient Greece was influenced by the Hebrew experience of God. Bennet challenged him to support this theory. Father Delaney then proceeded to say that the Greek traders went all over the Mediterranean and surely went to Palestine in their travels. While waiting for their ships to load and unload, they talked to the Hebrew merchants and learned that they had only one god. This was quite a novelty. No other people in the Mediterranean world had only one god. This god sometimes spoke to them and had given them laws which they felt compelled to obey or suffer the consequences. Their god protected them from their enemies if they lived their lives in accordance with his laws. The Greek traders had taken this information back to their homeland along with the textiles and other products they had acquired in Palestine. In conversations with their countrymen they spread the news about the Hebrew god and his commandments. These ideas filtered down into Greek literature and philosophy to the extent that Socrates, who believed in one god, was able to think up a philosophy that later suited Christianity.

Bennet said, "This speculation sounds all very well and good, Father, but there is no proof whatsoever for it."

"There is nothing in the written record. That's true. All of this was accomplished by word of mouth until finally it surfaced in the written word in Homer, Plato and others. Nonetheless, a natural law version of Christian ethics is clearly discernible in Greek thought."

"That could be merely a human development, Father. Nowhere is any credit given to the Hebrew way of thinking."

"Where did Socrates get the idea of one God?" Father Delaney asked. "There is nothing like that in Greek mythology."

"It just occurred to him. Where do we get any of our ideas?"

"That may be, but it is curious that it did not occur to the creators of religions who had no contact with the Hebrews. In fact, as the eddies of God's contact with His people got farther and farther from Palestine, less and less of the original inspiration appears. Thus the Hindus have many gods, the Buddhists have only an empty cosmology, and the Confucianists have only an ethics. The Greeks, on the other hand, in much closer contact with the Hebrews, have given us the literature and philosophy that underlie Christian civilization."

Bennet was disconcerted by this response, and the conversation turned into quieter channels.

As she approached the campus, Laurentia reflected on an insight she had had many years before. Almost immediately after her conversation with Aunt Melanie with respect to Bennet's emotional distance, she had come to the realization that she would have to live above the natural level. On the natural level she would not be able to find love. On that level only instinct and power "prowled about seeking the ruin of souls." Some marriages foundered between these rocks of Scylla and Charybdis, and Laurentia was determined this would not be her fate. Way back then she decided to insert love where it was not in the hope that she would receive at least a reflection of it.

Now she was worried that she was leaving her husband alone for too long; she wondered how he would manage without her. They had never been apart before for so long. He had gone abroad occasionally to attend conferences, but these had lasted for a week at most. He was talking of coming to Sydney during the semester break so perhaps that would suffice. As Stephen was staying with Aunt Melanie while attending university in Maynooth, she had no concern about him. Bennet was another story.

Ever since they had married, Laurentia had had a nagging thought in the back of her mind that she was only the first in a series of wives. She found herself looking around to see who might be her successor. It was a silly idea, but she could not let it go. Once she had paid a surprise visit to Bennet in his office at Trinity College and had walked in on a conference with one of his doctoral students, a Miss Christie Hanrahan. Miss Hanrahan was a striking blonde with an engaging smile. "Wife No. 2," surmised Laurentia. After that she did not visit Bennet at Trinity.

By now she had arrived at the university. She went to her lecture hall and arranged her notes. The first class went well. There were about a hundred students, and they seemed responsive. Laurentia felt her time in Sydney was going to be well spent. As she left the classroom, a casually-dressed older woman who introduced herself as Mary Oberst spoke to her about some things she had said in her lecture. They were still engaged in conversation as they left the lecture hall and walked together toward a campus cafeteria where they decided to stop for lunch.

Mary Oberst was from the States. She was in Australia because her husband's company had transferred him there. Only her youngest child was still at home. She had felt in need of some intellectual stimulation and so, as she had concentrated in French and Spanish in her undergraduate days, she was taking courses in the European Studies Program. Suddenly Mary leaned across the table and said confidentially, "I once knew a young man whose last name was Vann. We were practically engaged. He had had a difficult childhood, and it seemed to me that it had got the better of him." Laurentia reached for her coffee and tried to pretend indifference.

Mary continued, "Bennet Vann was his name."

Laurentia nearly spilled the cup of coffee she was maneuvering to her lips. "Whoops!" She made a joke of it. "Go on."

"Where was I? Oh yes, he had grown up in St. George, Utah. I suppose you have never heard of St. George."

"I have heard of it, but I don't know its significance."

"St. George is a little town in Utah where a sect of the Church of Latter-Day Saints rules the day. They practice Mormonism in all its primitive rigor, that is, they practice polygamy. Bennet grew up a child of polygamy. His mother was the third wife in his father's harem. In this community the elders banished well nigh three-quarters of the young men in order that those remaining might have multiple wives. After a young man he greatly admired was banished, Bennet realized his turn would be coming. He studied hard in school, thinking that soon he would have to make his way in the world and the more he knew, the better. When he was sent into exile by the elders, he headed across the border into Arizona and started life afresh. I met him in a French class at the University of Arizona in Tucson. We dated for a while, but he would never go to church with me. After his experience with the Latter-Day Saints, he had no interest in religion. He thought he could find what he needed in philosophy. When I saw that he really meant it, I threw him back in the pond, so to speak. I just wouldn't go out with him anymore. Then Tom, the love of my life, came along, and we have been happily married ever since. We have five wonderful children, and I couldn't be happier. I heard that Bennet went on to Stanford for graduate school, but then I lost track of him." Mary beamed as she said these words, and Laurentia could not doubt her happiness. The conversation then moved on to other topics.

Laurentia now understood her recurring nightmare. Bennet had been reared in polygamy. No wonder he would not discuss how many siblings he had; he made her look like an orphan. She shuddered to think how many graduate assistant lovelies were floating around him right then. The oxytocin would be running, and who knows what she might come home to. She wondered what would have happened if she had reacted as Mary did. Then she dismissed the thought. Her life was as it was, and she had to make the best of it.

In the following weeks Laurentia immersed herself in her class preparation and attended all the evening events scheduled by the European Studies Program. From time to time Sturmi Ziesel looked in on her, never failing to be solicitous for her welfare. She considered him to be a perfect gentleman and asked Monique about him. The Frenchwoman opined that he was a perennial bachelor; his mating instinct was dormant.

Laurentia did not forget Bennet in this heady atmosphere. She scoured the Internet for funny or idiosyncratic news and forwarded these items to him. When she spoke with him on the telephone, he was interested in what was happening to her but was reticent about his own activities. Laurentia had the impression that there was a great void in Dublin, a great dearth of interesting things to do and people with whom to converse. The emotional desert in which he was living never seemed so stark.

II

Restlessly Bennet Vann pushed his swivel chair back from the desk in his book-lined study at Trinity College and turned to stare despondently out the window. He had been going over the proofs for *The Soul of Western Civilization*, but now he gazed with a distracted air out into the distance. He seldom glanced at the vista of Dublin behind him so his fascination with it now was a measure of his discontent. For the moment he cared little about the philosophers brooding on the shelves around him, with arguments and refutations marshaled neatly according to author. Nor was he thinking about the articles, books and anthologies he had written and redacted which were shelved between Rousseau and Voltaire. He had not realized before what it was going to be like without Laurentia over the next couple of months. The laughter and intellectual excitement she had brought into his life had left him more or less permanently mellow. Now she was thousands of kilometers away, and he would not be seeing her until the semester break.

He remembered what the psychiatrist had told him in his undergraduate days. He had visited Dr. Foley because he felt vaguely depressed and could not put his finger on what caused it. He had never known how to assess the power situation in which he had been trapped as a child. He felt it was possibly still affecting him and making him unhappy. Then, too, he was angry about being banished from St. George by the elders.

Dr. Foley worked as a psychiatrist at the university's Counseling and Psychological Services. He ushered Bennet into an office whose décor consisted of diplomas and a couple of family photographs. Seated in a comfortable chair, Bennet unburdened his depression and his experiences to the psychiatrist and waited expectantly for his response.

"Many people emerge from childhood with an inner core of unhappiness," said Dr. Foley. "Since nothing in your current situation is causing you to be unhappy, we must conclude that your unhappy childhood is still impinging on your state of mind."

"What can I do about it?" Bennet asked. "Do I have to live with it for the rest of my life?"

"Certainly not," the good doctor replied. "You have to erase your anger at your parents and the elders or you will find yourself doing exactly the same thing."

"You mean I will have a harem?" Bennet was incredulous.

"Maybe not a harem but serial wives," answered the psychiatrist.

"How can I erase my anger?" asked Bennet.

"Don't think about St. George. Distract yourself whenever the thought comes to you. Fill your mind with happy thoughts," counseled the psychiatrist.

Bennet tried to take this advice and to distract himself from thoughts about his past, filling his mind with modern philosophy instead. In a course in Western civilization he came across Albert the Great who, the textbook informed him, was a man of encyclopedic knowledge. Bennet thought he would like to have encyclopedic knowledge too. This aspiration had taken him on to graduate studies at Stanford University and authorship and eventually a teaching position at Trinity College in Dublin.

Feeling a little depressed as he contemplated the vast stretch of time between late February and the middle of April, Bennet pondered what he should do. Almost two months in the doldrums was not a happy prospect. Just as he was contemplating the *néant*, Heather Graham, his teaching assistant, poked her head in the door. Heather was a pretty young thing with long golden locks.

"I know these aren't your regular office hours, Professor Vann," she opened, "but I wonder if I could discuss my dissertation with you." She was carrying a heavy tome.

Bennet decided to enforce the rules. He said, "I am busy at the moment, Heather. Could you come back tomorrow morning during office hours?"

"Certain, Professor Vann," she acquiesced and disappeared.

Bennet tapped his fingers nervously on the desktop and then grabbed his mobile phone. The dial tone rang a few times before an old voice crackling with energy came on.

"Hello, Vincent?" Bennet queried. On hearing an affirmative, he identified himself and said, "Say, Vincent,

Laurentia has gone down to Australia to teach a couple of courses.... Yes, she'll be gone until July.... The department chairman gave her no choice if she wanted to keep her job. What say we get together for dinner this evening?... How about the *Marco Polo*? Let me pick you up around 6:30.... Okay, see you then."

That had not been too difficult. Vincent was always good for an interesting conversation. Bennet began to look a little more serene as he went back to his proofs.

III

The day before Trinity College's semester break Bennet had a freak accident and sprained his ankle. He therefore spent the break at home instead of in Australia as he had planned. Vincent O'Malley dropped in for visits. When they heard of Bennet's debacle, church friends vied for the chance to share supper with him. Father O'Connor came a few times and kept Bennet in stitches recounting some of his adventures with eccentric parishioners. He always leavened his rapportage with a few intellectual tidbits so Bennet felt he was learning something in between laughs. Then, too, he talked to Laurentia every day and felt relatively cheerful. Aunt Melanie and Stephen came for a visit on Sunday. Bennet felt loved and was as content as could be expected under the circumstances.

The semester slipped away and *The Soul of Western Civilization* was published and met with critical acclaim. Bennet had been giving interviews on television and going to book signing parties.

Then July 5, the date for Laurentia to return from Sydney, arrived. Filled with anticipation, he drove out to the airport to meet the plane. He peered expectantly at the door from which he expected her to emerge. Suddenly he saw his wife, and his heart leapt within him. When they met, she hesitated a moment and gave him a quizzical look. He beamed in reply and had what he later could identify only as a mystical moment. "Laurentia!" he breathed as he leaned over to kiss her lightly. She put down her luggage and they embraced. The mystical experience evaporated and he turned to pick up her bags. They walked contentedly toward the door, her hand touching his arm.

Then she said with apparent nonchalance, "What have you been doing with yourself?"

"Do you really want to know?" he asked. "I could say wine, women and song, but actually it was more like O'Connor, Delaney and Friday nights at the Avila Retreat Centre listening to lectures on St. John of the Cross."

She laughed, and they returned to Donnybrook and an entirely different way of life.

Spanish Lessons

There are restaurants with minimal décor, and that was the situation of the Café Madrid, a little Spanish restaurant tucked away in a side street in Princeton, New Jersey. It catered to the university crowd – Spanish majors, Latin Americans feeling homesick, and an occasional professor and his consort. Every day a motley crew of casual passers-by also dropped in for a taste of Spanish cuisine. If they were looking for scenes of Madrid on the walls, they would be disappointed. The Café Madrid boasted only a pale interior in which table islands decked in wine-dark linens were arranged on a rug of a similar hue. At night vigil lights flickered on the tables, but that was management's sole concession to décor.

On Friday and Saturday nights the atmosphere became noticeably more authentic when a guitarist strolled among the tables and played softly on his instrument. Then the patrons had more of a sense of dining in Spain. When the guitarist Rafael Colón sang *canciones*, the clientele felt transported to Old Castile.

On a particular Friday evening in late February Deirdre McLaughlin slipped into the understated interior of the Café Madrid and was greeted by a smiling host. "Good evening, Señorita McLaughlin," he said and showed her to her usual table in the rear. Comfortably ensconced with a good view of the restaurant, Deirdre glanced over the menu, but she already knew that she would order the *paella a la marinera*. She was loath to embark on culinary adventures she might come to regret.

Alfredo came by and took her order. She lingered only over the choice of salad dressing but then decided on the Roquefort. She did not have to watch her weight. She was slender at age 29 and rather good-looking, with auburn hair and blue eyes. At her age Deirdre could afford to splurge on the Roquefort.

Rafael came out playing his guitar. This was the moment for which she had been waiting. She sat back and closed her eyes and let the music float into her brain. All week long she had been teaching biomedical engineering classes at Rutgers University so she rejoiced at the chance to unwind. Every Friday she came to the Café Madrid, ordered dinner and listened to Rafael sing Spanish songs. His *canciones* either excited her or lulled her into a dreamland of romance. Several months before, her friends had taken her to the Café Madrid for an evening out, and she was blown away by the guitarist and his music. Ever since then she had come every Friday night and had become acquainted with Rafael. He frequently spent his breaks at her table, conversing with her in Spanish.

They spoke of many things. Rafael worked in building maintenance at the Liberty Lane Retirement Community. His parents had a small *hacienda* in Colombia and had wanted him to study agricultural engineering. He had followed their wishes, but when he graduated, he realized he could not face life as a farmer. He had resolved the resulting impasse by coming to the United States to seek his fortune.

Sometimes Rafael talked about what it was like to live in Colombia, but mostly he talked about his adventures in building maintenance at the Liberty Lane Retirement Community. Some of the residents led singularly eccentric lives. Rafael had Spanish names for them all. He said if he did not laugh at their oddities, he might cry and he did not want to do that.

Deirdre was charmed by his conversation. It represented a complete change from the sedate professional world in which she usually moved. In the Biomedical Engineering Department at Rutgers everyone was careful to operate within certain bounds. Conversations outside the peer group never got personal. Even with the other professors conversations tended to be about professional matters with perhaps a nod to family life. The administrative staff was polite, calling her Professor McLaughlin. They observed the proprieties because they somehow sensed that their jobs depended on it. She was on a first-name basis with the other professors, but lurking in the background was the unspoken understanding that one's position depended on one's publications. In that respect Deirdre had nothing to boast about; she was low man on the totem pole. She was careful to refer to the director of the department, Professor Reynolds, by his title. He never corrected her, and most of the other professors used the honorific in his direction also.

For this reason Rafael was a refreshing change. He, too, had to watch himself during the day but let his guard down when speaking Spanish with her at night.

Rafael spoke a cultured Spanish and was happy to give her a few pointers. She also signed up for a class in night school to facilitate her conversations with him. She remembered her high school dream of one day living in

Latin America. Rafael, for his part, was delighted by her interest in his mother tongue.

Deirdre's father was a professor of microbiology at Princeton University and her older brother was a doctor. Deirdre decided to follow in their footsteps in the sciences and went into the field of biomedical engineering. She had thought she would one day get married and have children, but this dream had faded when she got to graduate school and the hard realities of taking examinations and doing creative research engrossed all her energies. She found that her classmates had worldly ambitions such as living in a mansion, driving around in an expensive car and vacationing in the Caribbean. They did not aspire to careers in the developing world. Deirdre absorbed the atmosphere around her and kept her nose to the grindstone. In graduate school it was a question of survival, and years of study had left her well-practiced in that.

When she received her doctorate, Deirdre found a teaching position at Rutgers University and moved back with her parents. As her parents had always been sympathetic to her, she did not have the centrifugal tendencies of her classmates. Longing for the day when they would be independent of their parents, they were careful to find employment some distance away from where their parents lived. Deirdre, on the other hand, moved home without a care in the world and in no time at all was completely absorbed in her teaching assignments.

That Friday night in late February Deirdre let the music lap around and envelop her. It was "*Arrivederci Roma.*" Her excitement climbed. She felt like dancing but confined herself to tapping her feet under the table. Then Rafael played "*Torna a Sorrento.*" When he finished, he smiled at her and headed in her direction. He sat down opposite her and cradled his guitar in his lap. She returned his smile and started off in Spanish.

"You are into things Italian tonight."

"Tonight I am in Italy." His eyes sparkled.

"This is the Café Madrid. We are supposed to be in Spain."

"My grandmother was from Italy. She taught me some songs when I was growing up and used to babble to me in Italian. Even now I can speak it in a crunch."

"Would you like to go there?"

"Yes. I have a cousin in Rome."

"Oh?"

"He's a priest. He teaches at the Angelicum."

He paused and Deirdre sensed he was feeling uncomfortable under her line of questioning.

She changed the subject. "So how are the residents at the Liberty Lane faring?" He laughed and told her about Romeo romancing Santa Catalina and Desafinado singing off-key in the shower early in the morning.

Later that evening Rafael sang a Colombian love song. Deirdre closed her eyes and let the words sink into her heart. A young woman introduced as Esmeralda danced the flamenco with castanets. Deirdre felt vaguely jealous of Esmeralda, but Rafael seemed to take no special notice of her. He seemed to sense Deirdre's reaction though and dropped by her table afterwards as if to assure her that Esmeralda represented only a professional relationship.

Once he asked her what she did for a living. She replied that she worked in a school. He said his sister did too and thought no more about it.

Another time she brought a friend with her – Raïssa Pavlov who taught psychology at Rutgers. That evening Rafael stayed away from her table, and Deirdre made a mental note to keep the Café Madrid separate from the rest of her life.

Then one Friday afternoon in March Professor Reynolds called her into his office. He told her that for now there was not enough work in the department to justify having so many teachers. As a consequence, he would have to let her go after the current semester. He wished her well and promised to give her a good reference. Deirdre was shocked. She had never expected this. She mumbled something, shook the proffered hand and managed to walk half-blind out of his office.

She had only one class that afternoon. Soon enough she found herself at home, pouring out the news to her mother.

"Don't worry, dear. I'm sure you will find something."

Unfortunately, her mother's assurances had no foundation in reality. It seemed that nothing was available that was close to home in biomedical engineering. She could find jobs as an adjunct professor of biology, but the salary was not enough to live on. Deirdre accepted two positions at small colleges for the fall and was happy that she could continue to live with her parents.

All this time she kept up her Friday night appointment at the Café Madrid but said nothing to Rafael concerning her troubles.

She met Raïssa Pavlov for dinner one evening and mentioned that she would be starting as an adjunct professor in the fall, but that was a stop-gap measure. She needed some advice. Raïssa queried her over her goals and her interests. Deirdre said she preferred teaching to research and did not want to leave Princeton. When Raïssa learned that Deirdre had become fluent in Spanish, she counseled her to widen her net. "Maybe you were meant to teach elsewhere."

Deirdre realized that if she wanted to find a job commensurate with her education, she would probably have to move. This was the state of affairs when she went to the Café Madrid on a Friday evening at summer's end.

She got caught in traffic and arrived a little later than usual. She had ordered the *paella* and had settled back to wait for it when she suddenly became aware that Rafael was not strolling about strumming his guitar as usual. She motioned to Alfredo. He moved toward her reluctantly, she thought. She asked him where Rafael was.

"Oh, he left," was the noncommittal reply.

"He left? What do you mean?" She was stunned.

"He went to Rome," Alfredo ventured.

"So when is he returning?" Deirdre wanted to know.

"I don't think he is returning."

Alfredo moved away while Deirdre meditated over the meaning of these words for a long moment before their impact settled in. Then she frowned and with a determined look on her face donned her shoulder bag and flounced out of the Café Madrid for the last time.

Win-Lose Games

Jaime Delgado was a thin man in his fifties, a professor of oncology at the medical school of Javeriana University in Bogotá. He was to be honored for his breakthroughs in cancer research that evening at the presidential palace. He fingered the invitation to dinner as he walked home from the laboratory that April afternoon. It was with some trepidation that he contemplated the engraved notice from the Palacio de Nariño inviting him and his spouse to the annual awards banquet celebrating the arts and sciences in Colombia. The Premios Colombia were to be distributed that evening, and Jaime was a surprised recipient.

Dinners and receptions at the presidential palace were far from his usual ambience. His normal trajectory lay between his home in an upscale neighborhood in the northern reaches of Bogotá and the oncology research laboratory at San Ignacio Hospital, a distance he covered on foot. It was on his peregrinations to and from his home that Jaime got his best inspirations. Somehow walking at a steady pace circulated blood to the brain and kept the inspirations flowing.

He could not have told you what lay along his route. He barely noticed the street signs and then only to direct his course. He missed the allurements of the shops lining the sidewalks. Lost on him were the colorful advertisements meant to attract passers-by. He left all such matters to his wife who was glad to oblige.

Jaime's single-minded adherence to his research endeavors had aided his marathon effort to find a solution to the mysteries of cancer. He let slip the traces of research only rarely, and receiving a Premio Colombia was one such occasion. Otherwise, he concentrated on facilitating a steady pace of small breakthroughs in the laboratory.

Jaime would have been the first to admit that he was driven by curiosity. When he formed a hypothesis or asked a new question, he was on tenterhooks until he got the answer. Sometimes the answers came overnight; other times he had to wait a few weeks or even months. Over time he had evolved into a world-class expert on cancer research and had become a sought-after speaker on the international conference circuit. This did not inconvenience Jaime because he was curious enough to want to know what others were doing. Traveling abroad to international conferences gave him a chance to pick their brains. Truth to tell, these oncologists formed an international mutual admiration society that lived for the epiphanies that research sometimes provided.

His wife Marta was okay with this *modus vivendi*. She was a cellist and had her string quartet and symphony orchestra to keep her busy. Jaime enjoyed listening to quartets so their house became the rendezvous for the group's Monday evening sessions. A few times a year Marta would play in a symphony concert, and Jaime was always in attendance. He liked having live music in his home. It gave a rounded, humane feeling to their hearth.

His two older children were off on their own now so the house was quieter than it had been. Only María, a medical student at Javeriana, still lived with them. Jaime was content to see that all three of his children had in one way or another taken after their parents. [Roberto]

With these thoughts Jaime swung along the sidewalk that led homeward. It was a Saturday afternoon, and he had been checking his experiments in the laboratory. He had left himself with a few hours to get ready for the presidential dinner, and then he and Marta would head downtown. She had told him this was an evening dress affair and had promised that she would see to the details. Jaime was content with this arrangement and abandoned himself to his oncological reveries.

At the other end of his stroll lay the apartment he and Marta had called home for the last few decades. His wife greeted him, all a-flutter at the thought of the evening that lay before them. She had laid out his evening clothes and was already dressed in a filmy pink gown. Jaime was happy to see her so excited. Marta lived more for social affairs than did he. He was glad he could offer her a few through his position as a professor at the medical school. This evening, he expected, would make medical school receptions pale by comparison.

A couple of hours later he found he was not disappointed in this expectation. When they arrived at the presidential palace, the guard saluted. Jaime looked around to see if there were a general or head of state in the vicinity. No, this was just the courtesy extended to every guest.

They were escorted into a glittering, chandeliered salon where the guests were to mingle before dinner. Looking around, Jaime realized he did not know a soul. Then a man and woman in their thirties approached and introduced themselves. It was José Rodriguez, a reporter for *El Tiempo*, and his wife María Teresa. He was to receive the Premio Colombia for journalism. Jaime congratulated him and told him of his own expectations. José was apparently not too interested in interviewing scientists because he went on to discuss a matter in his own field of political journalism. He said that politicians tended to find a *modus operandi* by means of which they could be successful. Then they stuck to that, whatever it was. So, for instance, a politician might think that he had to do something wrong to get ahead. Thereafter he would use this winning strategy and believe that this was what worked for him. Staying in office was hard work, the journalist opined, and some politicians had found that doing something wrong was efficacious. Until one day when they were caught and indicted and sent to jail for what they had done. Some of them managed to retire before they were caught. There were variations on this theme. One politician, for instance, thought that if she did what her superiors wanted, all ethical considerations aside, she would ascend the political ladder. So far this formula had worked for her, but she was beginning to run into heavy interference when she backed legislation that was unpopular with her constituents. José did not know how much longer the formula she had discovered would work for her. The journalist said he had rarely seen a politician change his *modus operandi*. They usually went down with the one they had previously found so effective. Apparently, they thought there was no point in changing horses in midstream, as the proverb goes.

    Throughout this monologue María Teresa had stood nursing her drink and smiling contentedly. When she saw a break in the conversation, however, she jumped in. "José has spent almost his entire life in Bogotá," she said, "but I was raised on a *hacienda* near Medellín. We were of the landed aristocracy dating back to the Spanish nobility who came in the sixteenth century. Yes, I am related to the Duchess of Alba." She paused to see how Jaime would react to that..

Jaime did not know how to reply to this information. He decided to say nothing.

María Teresa went on. "I was first tutored at home by a governess and then was sent to an exclusive boarding school in Bogotá. Eventually I went to UCLA because I have cousins living in Los Angeles." Again she paused and looked intently at him.

Jaime was perplexed as to how to reply. This was not a cancer question. "That's nice," he said.

At this point José caught sight of a friend and, making their excuses to Jaime and Marta, he and María Teresa moved away to a fresh conversation.

Jaime noticed that the president had entered the room and was working the crowd. He recognized him from his photographs. He wondered what formula the president used to ensure success in the unstable world of democratic politics. He had no time to turn this thought over in his head before an aide was telling the president that he was shaking hands with Jaime Delgado, the recipient of the Premio Colombia in Medical Science. The president spoke graciously to him and inquired after his activities on the international conference circuit. Then he smiled again and went on the next honoree.

After a while aides ushered the guests into the dining room. Jaime and Marta were escorted to their seats at the head table with the president. They found themselves sitting next to Martín and Elena Po. Martín Po was a novelist and was to receive the Premio Colombia in Literature. Jaime had never read his books and so had no clue as to what topics of conversation would interest him. As the dinner progressed, this did not seem to be a problem as Elena Po proceeded to recount their adventures on their travels around Europe. Jaime found himself laughing at some of the more outré episodes. Marta, too, was listening, and Jaime could see she was amused.

After dessert the president made a few remarks concerning the state of the arts and sciences in Colombia and then began to award the prizes. He asked each recipient to make a few remarks. Jaime wondered what he would say. He decided to be brief, simply thanking all the members of his research team who had made this recognition possible. Then he sat back to enjoy the occasion.

When Martín Po received the prize for literature, he recalled to the assembled guests that until recently literature in the Spanish language had been a miasma of tales of violence and dysfunctionality. This he ascribed to the dominance of the lower class in Spanish-speaking countries. Now, however, the middle class was dominant and therefore Spanish-language literature could expect a renaissance of fiction based on psychological themes. Personality, he said, characterizes the middle class – personality directed to strangers, family and friends. For this reason, Spanish literature was at the dawn of a new age when the emotional life of human beings would be explored. When he finished, the audience clapped a long time, and Jaime and Marta were not laggards in this respect. Jaime jumped to his feet and shook Martín's hand enthusiastically when he returned to his seat to show his appreciation of his remarks. Jaime thought that the dinner had been worth Martín's speech alone. They exchanged addresses when the reception was over and vowed to keep in touch. Jaime began to feel that there was a possibility that something of interest lay outside the oncology laboratory.

On Monday morning he was interviewed in his office by Laura Arroyo, a reporter from *El Tiempo*. Jaime had wondered what to expect and had decided just to answer her questions honestly. She could make of it what she wished.

The questions turned out to be relatively simple. How did you decide to get into research? Jaime told her that he had originally wanted to be a doctor with patients, but as he went through medical school, he was more and more drawn to research. By the time he was finished with his medical studies, he knew he wanted to teach and possibly do research if the opportunity presented itself. He was offered a teaching position at Javeriana and then just continued on there until the present.

Laura came back with a question about the international acceptance of his findings. Yes, he replied, they had been well received. He was always being invited to international conferences where scientists discussed their research. These conferences were a valuable source of new ideas and encouragement.

She asked if anyone had tried to stop him in his endeavors. Jaime was puzzled. She further explained, "Some people refer everything that happens in their social environment back to themselves. They are essentially egocentric, and they tend to compete with other people rather than love them. These people have a proclivity for playing win-lose games," she said. "This means that if you win, I lose. If I win, you lose. Politicians and athletes play win-lose games where one side wins and the other side loses. In other areas, however, most games are win-win games. If you win, I win. If I win, you win. This works in economics where cooperation and collaboration are rewarded. Some people, however, have learned to play win-lose games in childhood and are stuck in this mode." She looked at Jaime pensively. "I was just wondering if you had experienced anyone playing win-lose games with you, someone hoping you would fail."

"No, I can't remember anyone like that," Jaime answered. "Why would anyone want me to fail in cancer research?"

"It's not a rational thing," Laura explained. "It is just a reflexive competitive response to the environment."

"Have you ever felt that way?" he asked.

Laura replied in the negative. "The antidote to envy (because envy is what it is) is to think about all the blessings God has given you. In the spiritual realm you can think about all the graces He has bestowed on you," she replied.

That night her question came back to him before he drifted off to sleep. The next morning on his walk to the university a few memories floated into his head of occasions where someone or other had tried to stop his medical career. His father, for instance, had wanted him to stay on the *hacienda* and follow in his footsteps. His mother had then sent him to her brother, a Jesuit priest who taught physics at Javeriana University in Bogotá. As a young man, Jaime had yearned to be like his uncle. He had lived in a Javeriana dormitory near his uncle and had gone to San Bartolomé, a Jesuit *colegio*. Eventually he had won a scholarship to Javeriana itself.

Toward the end of his medical studies, Jaime had applied for a teaching position with research possibilities at various universities in Bogotá but received only the offer of a professorship at Javeriana. He recalled that he did not become angry when his hopes were initially frustrated. Then the miraculous had occurred, and he was invited to join the oncology research team at San Ignacio Hospital.

Then he remembered that in his first few years of research, before he had had any major successes, a colleague of his by the name of Jorge Padilla exhibited a certain competitive spirit. He was always telling Jaime about his uncle who was an executive at a chemical company in the United States. Jorge ignored or downplayed any successes Jaime had on the research front and sometimes gave him wrong advice on his research. Jaime did not "engage" with Jorge, that is, he did not confront him with his negativity; he just ignored it and went about his business. Except for Jorge, everyone else had been cooperative and encouraging. Jaime recognized also that he was too immersed in his research to have time to notice the negative behavior of other people.

Then Jaime remembered María Teresa and her wish to convey her superior status to him. Perhaps that was what was meant by a win-lose game. Now that her husband had won the Premio Colombia, she must surely be happy, he thought.

The Diablo Mystery

Ramona Preston was worried. She seemed to be landing assignments that were not demanding enough for her talents and ambition. She had refused to take a six-month assignment on the graveyard shift, and now she thought she was running the risk of being fired. She had thought that working after midnight with a minimum of social interaction with other employees was not something she would enjoy and she had declined the assignment, not realizing that it was not considered optional by top management.

Now it looked as if Agape International, a management consulting firm specializing in turnarounds, was getting impatient. All around her there were signs that she had to shape up or ship out. Her boss was a trifle short with her. The best assignments were being given to other associates. Ramona did not know what to do. The Depression was going full blast and finding employment other than in her family's cheese marketing business in Wisconsin was next to impossible. She realized she would have to make a special effort to redeem herself. And so she had volunteered.

In fact, she was not sure she could field the calls that might come in on the graveyard shift. Agape International was sure, however, and that was what mattered. She knew other people had done it before her so it was not impossible.

It was a question of staying up all night to monitor incoming calls from clients. Ramona would have to act as the first responder, that is, someone who was knowledgeable concerning all projects the firm was currently handling. She had to be ready to dispense advice or at least listen to problems in the middle of the night and notify the partners and associates concerned when they came in in the morning of changes in their clients' situations overnight. She was not allowed to take a nap while on duty. If she were caught doing so, she might be fired.

Ramona was a graduate of Marquette University and had a Master's degree in Business Administration from the University of Wisconsin – Madison. After she graduated, she worked as the director of marketing in her family's business of promoting Wisconsin cheese. Under her direction the company had doubled its sales, a circumstance which attracted attention at Agape, and she was hired.

She remembered the first time she had seen Agape's headquarters on Third Avenue in New York. She had walked into the paneled reception area and had seen a Japanese flower arrangement on the coffee table and immediately thought she would enjoy working for a firm that had such elegant taste. Away from the reception area, she learned, it was not so posh. Office décor featured drab off-white walls and sturdy metal desks except for a few partners' offices where individual taste reigned in a Persian rug or an antique desk. Ramona herself had not worked so far up the ladder that she could indulge in such amenities and, in fact, she did not feel any great desire to do so. Still, she admired others' good taste and was glad to work in such surroundings.

Ever since she had started at Agape International, her work life had been intense but rewarding. She loved figuring out good business strategies and felt that at Agape she was learning from the best management consultants in the country. The partners likewise had a high opinion of her and gave her interesting assignments. In this way she became familiar with almost all aspects of the firm's business with the exception of the most technical areas.

It was the graveyard shift that Ramona was not sure she could manage. Frequently nothing happened at all. There were hours on end when there were no calls. Clients knew the staff had gone home and waited until morning to contact the firm. That is, unless they had a real emergency.

At a certain point during the night Ramona thought boredom would settle in. She knew she had to try to stay alert on her own. Otherwise her job was over. She regarded a retreat to the family business as some sort of failure.

And so it was that at 11:00 p.m. on a Monday night in early October Ramona found herself starting her solitary duty on the graveyard shift. Almost everyone except Joe Lamb, the security guard at the reception desk, had gone home. Joe walked by every couple of hours so at least there would be occasional human company. Joe was an actor who, when he was in New York rehearsing, worked the graveyard shift at Agape. Every once in a while he left town on a tour with his troupe. He was an interesting conversationalist, having plenty of theatre yarns to tell which he punctuated with snatches of dialogue. Some of these were humorous excerpts from authors like James Thurber or songs from well-known musicals. Ramona admired him and thought of him as a person with a laugh inside.

The reception area, however, was far from the Situation Room where Ramona waited for incoming calls. At one end of the Situation Room was a table with communications equipment. The rest of the room was dominated by a massive oblong table with chairs. A few more chairs were placed at intervals along the walls. Ramona left her papers on the communications table and walked around the room. She sang a song. So far so good. Then the idea of sitting down and getting comfortable occurred to her. She knew that if she did that, she would probably fall asleep. Sitting down was a nonstarter.

Brendan Bonner, a man in his fifties, walked into the room. A recent widower, he had taken to staying late in the office. He told people he could get more done during the evening hours when the others had left for home. Still, he liked to take a break now and then, and when he saw Ramona, his face brightened.

"Oh, so you are here on an all-nighter," he commented. "How's it going?"

"Fine. Nothing's happening," she replied.

Brendan was not one for conventional chit-chat. "It was in just such a doldrums that we got a call about the Diablo Mystery," he responded. "That took a bit of extra cogitation since it was outside our usual expertise and came down to a matter of individual psychology and even diabolic interference."

"What are you talking about?" asked Ramona. "The Diablo Mystery? I never heard anything about that."

"It happened over ten years ago," Brendan replied. "At the time it was all very hush-hush. You must have heard about the Lithuanian airplane with the Lithuanian president and almost his entire cabinet as well as the country's top military brass on board that crashed in Russia so mysteriously."

"I vaguely remember hearing about it when I was in business school, but I never learned the details."

"It was an embarrassment to the Lithuanian air force so it was determined not to make a public statement. In addition, our ultimate conclusion could not be verified from the inductive point of view, which meant it would be unacceptable in certain circles. Thus our report was never made public. However, if you like, I will tell you the story. There can be no harm in it at this point."

"I would like to hear it." Ramona tried not to sound overeager.

"We were contacted by the Lithuanian air force which found itself unable to decipher what had transpired in the cockpit that had led to such disastrous consequences. They had had an earlier experience of our capabilities in another matter, and so they turned to us again for help. They wanted to make certain that no such eventuality could ever occur again."

Ramona nodded and he continued.

"I will recapitulate the circumstances for you. A Lithuanian air force plane was flying President Strazdas and his ministers, together with top military figures, to a meeting in Smolensk when it crashed in the fog surrounding the airport there. The crew had not been together long and was not trained for flying in unusual circumstances. In other words, the crew members had not had time to develop a strong rapport with each other. Likewise, they did not have any training about what to do in emergencies. The plane was in excellent condition and so there was no question of any malfunction in its systems."

Brendan paused for a moment. "So what happened?" Ramona nudged him, figuratively speaking.

"The control tower had told the pilot to go elsewhere as the fog in Smolensk was too dense for a safe landing. The pilot should have followed the control tower's instructions. Why didn't he? That was a big question. The black box recovered after the crash revealed that there had been a visitor to the cockpit during the approach to the Smolensk airport. Voice analysts identified him as the general commanding the air force. The tape revealed that he urged the pilot to land despite the fog that was reported on the ground."

"Did the pilot have to obey the general?" Ramona wanted to know.

"No, it was a wish rather than a command. Ultimately, the pilot was the decisionmaker."

"How did he make his decision?"

"There were other inputs. A Russian plane radioed the Lithuanian plane that they had made two attempts at landing but found the fog too dense and were going elsewhere. A Lithuanian air force plane that had landed an hour and a half earlier told the presidential plane that conditions on the ground had considerably deteriorated since it had touched down. The fog was denser now. Nonetheless, the pilot of the presidential aircraft decided to land. Twice an automated voice told the crew in the cockpit that there was "terrain ahead," a clear warning that they were flying too close to the ground. The pilot did not react to these danger signals but left the plane on automatic pilot. Why did he not react? Why did he not do the obvious thing in order to survive? Eighteen seconds before the crash occurred, the automated voice said "pull up." The pilot waited 13 seconds and then banked the plane for a fresh attempt at landing. In other words, he did not follow the instruction to "pull up" but turned sideways. The question is, why did he not pull up first and then attempt a fresh landing? Five seconds after he changed direction, the plane hit a tree. Just before that someone in the cockpit started praying and the others started screaming. Evidently, they finally saw how close they were to the ground."

"So it was a question of pilot error?" asked Ramona.

"Yes, but why did he make such an egregious error? That is the real question and the one worth answering so that this sort of accident can never happen again."

"Could it have been suicide? Was the pilot depressed?"

"No, that possibility had to be ruled out. He was for all intents and purposes a happily married man with three children. There was nothing in his background that would indicate depression or suicidal tendencies."

"Then what induced him to make such an error in judgment?" asked Ramona.

"I had to go to deductive reasoning as the evidence had taken us as far as it could. Deductively, I could surmise that the pilot had some difficulty following orders. He failed to respond to the control tower, the advice of the crews of two planes in the vicinity, and his training. He knew that he was the ultimate decisionmaker. Nonetheless, he ceded his responsibility to the air force general who wanted to land. In the face of obvious danger he persisted in trying to carry out the wishes of the general."

"Why would he do that?" asked Ramona, trying to be patient.

"The general had the ability to promote him. The pilot dismissed advice from all other quarters, including the warning messages from the airplane's computers, and blindly obeyed the wishes of the general. Knowing a little psychology, I can surmise where he was coming from."

"Where?" asked Ramona, feeling naïve.

"The evidence suggests that the pilot did not like to follow orders. In other words, he had a problem with vertical relationships. He resolved this difficulty by slavishly obeying people in a position to promote him. He hoped thereby to go up the ladder and ultimately to have no one or very few people in a position to give him orders. He had what I call a Führer fixation. He obeyed his leader without thinking. This ultimately led to his destruction and the deaths of all those on board the plane he was piloting."

"That explanation seems to fit all the constraints of the data available," observed Ramona.

"Wait, there is more." She looked at him quizzically. "I started wondering how an experienced pilot could have acted according to the Führer fixation when death was staring him in the face. Did he have a death wish? Had he somehow overridden the survival instinct? I came to the conclusion that while he might have had a Führer fixation, something else was interfering with his judgment. Someone was putting wrong ideas in his head. Faced with three automated warnings and the imminent possibility of death, he was truly acting irrationally in disregarding them, and I did not want to accept that explanation."

"So what else could have been interfering with his judgment?" asked Ramona, surprised by the ongoing mystery.

"I could readily believe that someone was interfering with his thought processes and telling him to land in spite of everything. A voice in his head was forcefully reiterating that landing the plane in the fog would be a great feat and would win him a promotion."

"He heard this in his head?"

"Yes, I think the devil was putting ideas in his head that would make a plane crash happen."

"Wow!" exclaimed Ramona.

"It is pretty extraordinary, but the facts in this case are extraordinary so I had to look beyond obvious explanations. At any rate, all I can be certain of is that the disaster had the devil's fingerprints on it. That is why I call it the Diablo Mystery. This explains the pilot's nonresponse and tardy and incorrect response to the automated messages. He considered that he was in great danger, but then the devil intruded the thought that if he landed the plane in the fog, he would win a promotion. Having no consideration for the safety of his crew, men he hardly knew, he decided to go for the promotion and in the end steered the plane sideways instead of up. In fact, I am convinced that if the devil had not been present at this decisionmaking moment, the pilot's concern for his own survival would have dominated his thinking and he would have taken the plane to a higher altitude and sought to land elsewhere. His hesitation shows that a stronger suggestion was being made."

"This interpretation was never made public."

"There are elements in society that resist the deductive method of reasoning. They also do not recognize the existence of the devil. For this reason after I told the Lithuanian air force my conclusions, they were never made public."

Ramona had another thought. "Is there any defense against the devil introducing wrong ideas into people's heads?"

Brendan hesitated. "Well, the devil can introduce an idea into your head, but if you recognize it as an alien thought and not simply a new idea, then you will not entertain it but will continue to think your own thoughts. In this case the pilot could have rejected the general's suggestion in light of the danger involved. He could have reverted to his training. Any suggestion from the devil that a successful landing would win him a promotion could have been cast aside as an alien idea. Survival mattered most. One's training should override any counsels from the devil."

"One last question," Ramona said. "How can one guard against diabolic interference? How could President Strazdas and the others have ensured their safety?"

Brendan hesitated. "You mean other than allowing only people who take Judaeo-Christian principles and professional norms seriously to become airplane pilots? Well, the passengers could have included a few exorcism prayers in their daily conversations with the Almighty."

A call was coming in from a client and Ramona turned to answer it. Brendan smiled in her direction and disappeared down the hall.

One o'clock in the morning came and went. The idea to sit down occurred to her again. "If I sit down, I had better keep busy and not fall asleep," she said to herself. "That is *verboten*." She knew Brendan was long gone. If it were not for the company policy against dating, she could well imagine interesting dates with Brendan. If a romantic interest were detected by the firm, however, both parties would be instantly fired. This served to keep Agape International businesslike and professional. Especially in the midst of the Depression no one wanted to take any chances with his or her job. Ramona dreamt about a possible romance, but she knew such a relationship was next to impossible. She would have to leave her job immediately in order for dating to occur.

Singing songs quietly, Ramona managed to feel wakeful. It seemed now a question of lasting until dawn, at which time she could leave and go to a coffee shop for breakfast. A few more hours would do it.

She called a friend who lived in Tokyo. Her adrenalin started flowing in the excitement of the conversation. She typed out a couple of e-mails. She took a call and dispensed some advice. She felt successful. Then in her great happiness she sat back in her chair and relaxed.

The Reunion

Adriana Briant had left her husband, children and grandchildren in Houston and had flown up to Washington, D.C. to reconnect with the Alma Mater she had graduated from forty-five years previously. She had spent the afternoon wandering around the Georgetown University campus trying not to get lost. So many new buildings had been added since her undergraduate years that she was constantly having to ask for directions. Fortunately, everyone understood that she was a distressed alumna on campus for the Reunion Weekend and was glad to give remedial assistance. The campus had been reinvented over the past forty-five years, and Adriana felt as clueless as any freshman arriving for orientation. Spaces where green fields had once provided expansive vistas suited for athletic pursuits as well as meditation were now busy with modern architecture. At length, after wandering around the imposing new Intercultural Center and locating the Epicurean Club and other posh watering holes, Adriana decided to visit Dahlgren Chapel. That, at least, was as she remembered it.

She was almost alone in the chapel. After noting a certain prominence donor Elizabeth Dahlgren had given to her patron saint, Elizabeth of Hungary, in the stained-glass windows, Adriana slid into a back pew and said a prayer that her husband and her children and her grandchildren would be safe and well in her absence. She then went on to commend her entire acquaintanceship to the benevolent concern of the Almighty. Adriana had a large acquaintanceship and had only barely begun her commendations when she was distracted from her prayers by the question of what she could expect over the next few days.

Examining the list of her classmates who had signaled their intention of attending the reunion, Adriana felt a bit disconcerted. She had transferred to Georgetown in her junior year and therefore had to make up some required courses so she did not make many friends in her academic year. Most of the ones she remembered from the School of Foreign Service, her undergraduate college, were not attending the reunion. Only Lee Thompson, someone she knew from the Philodemic Society, the debating club, was more than a name to her. Reunions were every five years; she would not know anyone in the other reunion cohorts. She had signed up for the class party on the first night so she made a mental note now, sitting in the chapel, to be on the lookout for Lee that evening. Otherwise she feared she would be socializing with strangers.

If the campus had been reinvented in the last forty-five years, Adriana knew she had been reinvented also. She was no longer the quiet, studious young woman she had been in her undergraduate days; she had blossomed into a relatively outgoing individual with interests beyond history and foreign languages. How this had come about she was not entirely sure but was certain it had something to do with falling in love with her husband John. That marvelous event had awakened all sorts of personality and other outcomes in her and had determined the course of her life from that time on.

Along with John, her children – Joanna, Adrian and James – and her grandchildren were the center of her attention now. She had, nonetheless, kept up her credentials as an intellectual by taking courses at Rice University. Her husband John, a physicist at the Houston Space Center for many years and now retired, had stepped in as a babysitter whenever she was gone. He was not a cook so he and the children went out for dinner when she was not around. In this way they had developed a certain taste for Mongolian cuisine and had found occasion to practice their Spanish. The children were content with this arrangement although they generally preferred their mother's cooking. Now the same pattern was continuing with the grandchildren who were getting used to dining in exotic ambiences.

It was five o'clock – time to register at Alumni House and pick up her weekend schedule and name tag. She looked around the chapel once more at the figures in the stained-glass windows and then slipped out the door.

The staff at Alumni House was cordial and soon fixed her up with the weekend's necessities in a Georgetown University tote bag. Her class party was getting under way at *Martin's Tavern* on Wisconsin Avenue so Adriana decided to repair there next and not be fashionably late.

She mused on these and other matters as she walked to the tavern on the red brick sidewalks that flowed past the eighteenth and nineteenth century townhouses characteristic of the Georgetown section of Washington. Upon her arrival, she was ushered into a corner where fellow alumni were sporting similar identification tags and tote bags. All were strangers to her; she realized she might spend her evening mixing with strangers. Nonetheless, she waded into the conversation and discovered in short order that she was in the company of alumnae from the School of Nursing. This clique was invaded by a pack of old boys from the College, another group that was busy reconnecting with unfamiliar faces. Someone from the School of Foreign Service saw her name tag and started a conversation. He mentioned that a classmate was now the ambassador to Senegal. Adriana contributed that another classmate had become the abbess of a Trappistine convent in Indonesia and yet another was the mayor of a town on Long Island. When she did not mention any titles indicating her own managerial accomplishments, her new-found classmate lost interest in the conversation and wandered off again.

Adriana waited to see if the opportunity for another conversation would present itself. When it did not, she decided it was time to go. As she inched toward the door, she remembered to keep her eyes open for Lee. A silver-haired lady was passing who looked vaguely familiar. "Are you Lee Thompson?" she asked hesitantly. "Yes," replied the elderly version of Lee. "Oh, I am so glad to see you!" exclaimed Adriana. "You were practically the only person on the list of those who were coming that I knew. I remember you from the Philodemic Society debates on Sunday evenings. You had so much to say and I could not say anything. I had stage fright back then and besides I had no opinions on the matters being debated. You always took the liberal side of every question, and Regis McBride took the conservative side. I would sit spellbound in the back row. I found it exciting just to listen."

"I don't know you," said Lee.

Adriana laughed. "It is not surprising that you don't remember me. I was always so quiet. I could not speak in public then. I can now. Some people are late bloomers." Lee still had a puzzled expression on her face. Adriana talked a while longer and then made her excuses and left. On the way to her brother's apartment in Friendship

Heights, courtesy of the D.C. transit system, she thought over her conversation with Lee. She laughed to herself that she had so looked forward to reminiscing with Lee who did not even remember her. That was so funny! She wondered if her looks had changed that much in forty-five years. She thought she would have fun telling John about it when he called that evening.

On the following day Adriana went to a seminar on Carroll Quigley which her brother, a professor of European history, had initiated. Quigley had taught a required course in ancient history when Adriana was an undergraduate. A few decades before the reunion he had gone to his eternal reward, but he had left a lasting impression on his students. For this reason the seminar in Riggs Library was packed. Her brother and other professors shared their impressions of Quigley and then the floor was opened up for comments from the audience. Quigley had had some interesting ideas on the rise and decline of civilizations. For instance, he thought that every once in a while a civilization would enter a period of Conflict. From this it would emerge either into an era of Universal Empire or an era of Expansion. If the former, then it was doomed to extinction. Fortunately, Western Civilization had always emerged from Conflict into a period of Expansion. Ideas such as these had made a lasting impression on his students; the audience was crammed full of strong memories. Thus audience recollections varied from comments on impossible exam questions to memories of occasions when Quigley was actually manhandled by his students on account of his controversial opinions. As these comments and others generated considerable emotional excitement, when the clock forced the session to conclude, the room burst into excited conversation. Adriana looked around and found Lee waiting for her. "I remember you," Lee smiled in triumph and opened an old yearbook, pointing to Adriana's photograph.

"That was my best picture," Adriana replied. Once more the thought that both she and the campus had changed crossed her mind. Unfortunately, while the campus looked a little newer, she looked a little older. Nonetheless, she knew that the biggest change had come in her personality. She was simply a happier, more interesting person than she had been as an undergraduate.

"So what have you been doing with yourself?" Lee wanted to know. "I remember you went off to Stanford for East Asian Studies or some such."

"Yes," chuckled Adriana. "And I met my husband there. He retired as a project manager of space flights at the Space Center in Houston a few years ago although he still does occasional consulting work. We have three children and now have seven grandchildren. I have helped my husband out at international conferences when he has to interface with foreign scientists and engineers. And I have a Master's degree in Social Psychology from Rice University and sometimes still take courses there."

"So you went to Stanford in East Asian Studies and ended up as a housewife?"

Adriana thought she detected a disdainful note in Lee's voice. She decided to change the subject. "So what have you been doing?" she asked.

"I got my doctorate from Princeton in political science and now teach at the University of Michigan."

"Wow! That's terrific!" Adriana exclaimed.

"Yes," Lee agreed. "I have published some monographs on the sociology of American electoral politics and have won some recognition in the field. But how could you go from being someone who was interested in foreign service to being a housewife?" There was a tone of incredulity in her voice.

"I guess meeting John changed me." There was a pause. Then Adriana considered that the best defense was a good offense. "Are you married?" she inquired.

"No, I am happily unmarried."

Adriana wondered if Lee had ever been in love, but she decided she did not have to ask. She knew the answer already.

"When women walk away from careers and get on the Mommy track," observed Lee, "they make universities reluctant to accept women in their programs."

"But look at the number of men who change fields. Even in our own class at the School of Foreign Service, Paul Gannon became a member of the diocesan clergy."

"You're kidding! How do you know that?"

"I read it in the newspaper when he was ordained for the Houston Archdiocese. People don't always end up in the field they studied. This allows for cross-fertilization of areas of expertise."

"It is hard to see how Paul is going to use his knowledge of international economics and U.S. diplomatic history in his assignments as a priest," remarked Lee.

"Not everyone knows what he wants to do in life when he attends college," Adriana observed.

At this point someone she did not recognize came over and started a conversation with Lee so Adriana took her cue and made an exit.

On her way back to her brother's apartment that evening Adriana reflected on Lee's comments and body language. She knew that attending the School of Foreign Service had been a mistake on her part. She had enjoyed her French and Spanish classes in high school so her father had envisioned that she might become an ambassador or something of that sort. Adriana mused that she would have been better off in a women's college preparing for what ultimately was to become her career. I am where I am supposed to be, she thought. John and my children and grandchildren need me. They need to be loved, and I'm it. She smiled to herself and resolved to talk to strangers for the rest of the weekend.

The Tragedy of Cyber Contra

    Life had been pretty much a bowl full of cherries for Wulphy Mireau up until his current assignment at Phelps Cybernetics. He had grown up in the cathedral town of Lewiston, Maine and had enjoyed a happy family life. He had then gone away to M.I.T. where he had worked his way through an undergraduate major in mathematics and a Master's degree in Information Technology. At a conference on John Henry Newman at Boston College he had met Marie, a student of European history at that institution. When they graduated, they celebrated their wedding in Boston College's chapel. After a memorable honeymoon in France, they moved to Mountain View, California where Wulphy had secured a plum job at Phelps Cybernetics. Wulphy thought he had the best of all possible worlds: a job with challenges and some hope of upward mobility and a wife who loved him and made life a window on heaven.

    Wulphy worked in the Phelps Building in downtown Mountain View. In the lobby an outsized glass statue of a man strode along with his gaze fixed upward.

On the surrounding walls were equations and Greek letters. Whenever Wulphy entered the lobby he felt an uplift from the intellectual vistas it suggested. It was well that he experienced euphoria from the lobby because the offices on the floors above were strictly utilitarian. Beyond a flower arrangement in the reception area on each floor, the company made no further concession to aesthetics. Wulphy was jerked back to reality and the task at hand as soon as he left the lobby.

    He was balancing between the euphoric and the down-to-earth rational mind one morning when he found a note from his manager, Drithelm Woods, among the messages that had accumulated overnight in his e-mail. He was to come in first thing in the morning so they could talk. Not knowing what to expect, Wulphy gathered a few papers, said a little prayer, and covered the ground between his office and Drithelm's corner office with an alacrity that could only be described as "making haste slowly." Drithelm greeted him warmly and motioned him to a seat. It took the older man about a minute to get to the point, Wulphy balancing on the edge of his seat and clutching his papers all the while. It seemed that his work had found favor in high places, and he was being transferred to Cyber Contra effective the following Monday. He was assured that this was a promotion. The management team at Phelps was so happy with his work thus far that they felt they could pass him on to the troubleshooting going on in Cyber Contra, that is, the defense of clients against cyberattacks. In his new position his supervisor would be Ahmad Karzai, a computer whiz from Afghanistan who had studied at Caltech. Phelps wanted to underscore the nature of this promotion by giving him a substantial boost in pay. He would find it in his next paycheck.

    Wulphy was overwhelmed. That evening he rhapsodized to Marie about it. "Just think! I have been here only six months and already they are giving me one of the most difficult assignments."

Marie smiled but interposed, "I suppose they will want you to put in more hours. Who knows what time you will be getting home!" Wulphy had to agree with her but thought such a change in his hours would have happened sooner or later anyway. Having a lot of free time was one of the things a man had to give up if he wanted to get ahead.

It was with such happy thoughts that he reported to Ahmad Karzai the following Monday morning. When he entered Ahmad's office, a middle-aged man of medium build rose from behind his desk and shook his hand, then waved him to one of the steel chairs upholstered in black to match the carpet. Wulphy sat down and proceeded to listen to a summary of the difficulties a client, Microflash, Inc., had been having with malware in the last month. Then Ahmad gave him a memorandum on the subject and invited him to attend a mid-morning conference with the client. Wulphy smiled his assent and left Ahmad's office feeling that his new assignment was going to be interesting. He hoped he was up to the challenge.

A week later he was not so sure. Ahmad was constantly criticizing his work. It seemed he could do nothing right. When he mentioned this to Ed Wright, an older colleague who was working on the same assignment, Ed assured him that it was simply Ahmad's way of handling his subordinates. Wulphy resolved to grin and bear it, especially when he considered that everyone was experiencing the same kind of treatment.

Then Wulphy began to notice that Ahmad seemed to be giving him some special attention. Ahmad told him every time Boston teams lost a game. Thus Wulphy learned about all the defeats the Celtics and the Bruins suffered. When baseball season arrived, he heard about every game the Red Sox lost and was surprised to find out at the end of the season that they had won the pennant. In fact, Ahmad kept him up to date on all negative happenings in the Bay State and Down East. One day he confronted Ahmad about his negativity just to see what his reaction would be. "You are telling me all the bad news you can about Massachusetts and Maine," he said.

Ahmad smiled. "No, I am just keeping you current so that when you go home for a visit, you will be in the swim. You will know all the news." That rejoinder shut Wulphy up for a while.

When the Red Sox won the pennant, though, he thought he would mention it to Ahmad. "After all the terrible news about Red Sox' defeats, how could they win the pennant? I can't understand it."

Ahmad said he could not understand it either. They both smiled and left it at that.

Wulphy began to consider his relationship with Ahmad a game. He fantasized that Ahmad was readying him for happy surprises down the way: the world was not going to come to an end, California was not going to slide off into the ocean, the United States was going to muddle through its economic difficulties. By telling him all the bad news, Ahmad was really his best friend, making sure his life would be full of happy surprises.

Somehow Wulphy sensed that he could not repay Ahmad in kind. If he were to say anything negative about Afghanistan, his boss would return to the attack with a vengeance. To put it simply, he could not retaliate or he would have no job. He resolved to continue to construct humorous fantasies about Ahmad so as to erase any negative feelings that might otherwise collect around this relationship.

After a while, however, Wulphy began to feel sorry for himself. He became despondent and even depressed. When Ahmad's father died, Wulphy felt what he later came to term "the thrills." He knew it was wrong to enjoy someone else's pain. This must be what they call *Schadenfreude*, he thought.

He began to experience the thrills whenever someone was in emotional or physical pain. He did not think there was anything wrong with this because he was not causing the pain. He was just having a thrill. He was so despondent most of the time that he thought having thrills was somehow okay. In fact, his despondency he began to label "the horrors," a state of mind that was so depressing he would not wish it on his worst enemy.

Around this time Marie started taking evening courses in Modern European History at the University of Santa Clara. She would arrive home around ten o'clock at night when Wulphy was ready to turn in for the night. In any case, he did not feel he could confide in Marie about what was happening. In fact, she had not studied psychology and could not be expected to have any particular insights. When this had been going on for a few months, he thought he had better visit a psychiatrist to find out what was going on.

Raymond Collins was someone Wulphy had met in church. He thought Dr. Collins was a regular guy and would probably be a good bet for figuring out what was wrong with him and what to do about it. Thus he found himself making an appointment for the following Thursday evening.

After listening to Wulphy's description of the circumstances of his emotional life, Dr. Collins had a few suggestions. "First of all," he said, "if you want to stop having the horrors, you have to be willing to give up the thrills. They are related. Every time you experience a thrill, know that a horror will subsequently occur."

"How can I stop a thrill?" Wulphy wanted to know.

"Just suppress it when it starts up. You can do that," replied the doctor.

"Anything else?" Wulphy asked.

"And secondly, make sure you never feel sorry for yourself. That's how you got into this psychological trap."

"That's easier said than done," replied Wulphy.

"It seems to me you were initially doing a pretty good job of maintaining your happiness level by making up all those humorous fantasies as to Ahmad's motivation. Just keep fantasizing along those lines. Who knows, maybe you can write a book about Ahmad's great kindness toward his fellowmen."

Wulphy laughed. "Thanks, Dr. Collins. I'll do my best."

"It's Raymond to you. I have the feeling our relationship will be purely social from now on, but if you have any more difficulties, give me a call."

Wulphy was delighted with this outcome and put Dr. Collins' advice into practice. His old *joie de vivre* returned. He even started perking Ahmad up by recounting to him humorous anecdotes he had picked up on the Internet. Ahmad started to break into a smile as soon as he saw him and the old negative stories about Boston sports teams ceased. Ahmad praised his work to other managers. In fact, he came to regret this because a certain vice president took notice and had Wulphy transferred to his unit. Ahmad cried a little and told Wulphy how much he would be missed. Wulphy assured him that they would continue to see each other at company affairs, if not in the cafeteria. Thus what began as the tragedy of Cyber Contra ended up in comedy.

The Colombian Eight Escudos Piece

On a Tuesday morning in April, when the parks were beginning to boast green lawns and successive waves of spring flowers after lying dormant all winter, the Metropolitan Museum of Art was bustling with amateur art connoisseurs. Among these were Mary Stadeck and Claire Martin who had come in from the suburbs to view a special exhibit of medieval tapestries. Strolling from room to room with headsets and audio equipment, they examined the tapestries with a sharp eye for detail. Upon completing the tour, they repaired to one of the dining areas, acquired a gourmet chef's version of ham and cheese sandwiches, and found a table near a fountain.

Sitting beside a satyr dancing under a light shower, Mary waxed enthusiastic over the tapestries they had just viewed. In particular, she admired the unicorn series on loan from the Cloisters Museum. Claire nodded at her commentary, but her thoughts seemed to be elsewhere.

When Mary expatiated on the different layers of meaning in the unicorn tapestries, Claire interpolated, "It's interesting that you mention different layers of meaning because something like that has been happening in my life lately. With each new discovery, my perspective on what is occurring has changed." She paused and Mary encouraged her to continue.

"Something is happening at my husband's firm these days, and it has been puzzling us a great deal. I remember you solved the mystery of lights playing in a deserted house in Wuthering Lane and you puzzled out how thieves had managed to steal a Rembrandt from the Westerbrook Collection so perhaps you might have some ideas concerning this." She looked at Mary expectantly, hoping to receive an affirmative reply.

"I will try. If the situation is not hopelessly opaque, perhaps I can figure it out."

Thus reassured, Claire said, "First, you must promise to keep it a secret." Mary agreed, and her friend continued. "Christopher, as you know, is a partner in a financial firm which, among other things, deals in numismatic coins. While he is chiefly involved in the business end, the numismatics division is under his jurisdiction so what has occurred is in his area of responsibility. That is why he is most troubled by recent losses there, one involving a Colombian eight escudos piece worth over $10,000."

Claire paused to take a sip of water, and Mary seized the opportunity to ask her what security precautions were in place. "On account of the great value of the inventory," Claire continued, "the numismatic division is subject to special security precautions. A bulletproof window separates customers from the staff, and the work area may be reached only through a series of doors which are electronically controlled. These may be opened only by the staff from the inside. The security of the area is further enhanced by the fact that all prospective employees must submit to a lie detector test. Some ex-police officers authorized to wear revolvers are on the staff. Each week a portion of the inventory is counted so that the absence of any coins would be detected within, at most, three weeks. At night the inventory is locked away in the vault. The combination on the lock cannot be touched before morning without setting off alarms. In addition, there are electronic surveillance units designed to detect anything moving around the office at night, also activating the alarms. These units have never gone off since they were installed a few years ago. All of this security, while it sounds impressive, is required by the high value of the inventory. From time to time there have been attempted break-ins when the office is open so the staff is always alert to the possibility of such."

Her friend commented, "It sounds like a very complete security arrangement."

"It is, and that is what has Christopher so baffled. At the last accounting for gold the Colombian eight escudos coin was missing. The standard lie detector test was administered but revealed nothing. The first facile explanation that occurred to us was that it was a question of faulty accounting, that is, the coin had been sold without being recorded. It is impossible, however, that the numismatists on the staff not recollect that such a piece had been sold. So the first two explanations, that someone on the staff took it or that it was sold without the sale being recorded, have been discounted. New theories have come to the fore, namely, that the coin was lost somewhere in the office or someone had absent-mindedly put it in his pocket and carried it home. A thorough search of the office negated the first theory, and my husband is now considering administering another lie detector test to see if someone had inadvertently taken the coin home and then failed to return it upon discovering it later. He has notified other numismatic firms of the loss, but so far no one has come forward to report a sale or an attempted sale of the missing coin. So, you see, all of this leaves Christopher with quite a problem. It is too large a loss to be ignored, and his partners are insisting that he solve the mystery without delay."

"It sounds intriguing," Mary commented. "I would like to survey the scene of the crime, if I may." Claire thought that could be arranged. She phoned her husband and told him they would drop by the numismatic division for a visit.

Having finished their lunch, the two friends left the museum and made their way to the midtown business district. They arrived at the numismatic division of Hadley, Ryland & Martin in an underground shopping mall about twenty minutes later. A staff member recognized Claire and allowed the two women to pass through the electronic doors. Thus ushered into the office area, they surveyed the scene. An apparent confusion prevailed, employees milling about in a seemingly random fashion. Telephones were ringing, prices were being quoted and orders taken. Numismatists carried their precious inventory into cubicles where they negotiated with sophisticated clients in a leisurely fashion. The vault stood off to one side, its door open for the day's business. At this point their observations were cut short by the appearance of Christopher Martin.

"Claire! Mary! I am delighted to see you. I knew you were coming into the city today, but I did not anticipate that you would honor us with a visit."

"After we finished viewing the tapestry exhibit, we had some extra time so we came here," said his wife by way of explanation.

"I'm happy to see you. Would you like me to show Mary around the office?"

"Please do," murmured his wife.

Thereupon Christopher Martin guided the two women around, pointing out the walk-in vault, the electronic surveillance units, and the buttons for opening the electronic doors. Into none of this conversation did the topic of the mysterious loss intrude although the two women did ask a few pointed questions about the equipment, employee security, and accounting procedures. Mary, in particular, was fascinated by the walk-in vault, examining its interior with care. She also observed closely the office walls, ceiling and floor, taking special heed of the area commanded by the electronic surveillance units. Their tour accomplished, the women thanked their guide and bade him farewell.

"What do you think?" Claire queried when they emerged onto the sidewalk.

"I am not sure," Mary rejoined. "It is all quite baffling." On this note the conversation turned to other topics.

The following morning Claire phoned Mary with the news that when the staff had counted the silver inventory on the previous evening, they discovered that several other rare coins were missing. Claire's voice had a frantic note.

"Do you think Christopher would mind if we discussed this with him?" Mary asked.

"No, of course not. At this point he would be happy to have an outside opinion," Claire responded. "Why don't we go into the city and have lunch with him?"

Mary assented to this proposal and accordingly the two women found themselves a few hours later sitting with Christopher Martin in the *Napoli* restaurant near his office.

"I am willing to listen to any theories you might have as to the disappearance of these coins," opened Christopher.

Mary replied, "Since your security setup seems impregnable, the only answer left is that one of the employees has stolen the coins. However, they have all passed the polygraph test with no trouble. Polygraph tests can be beaten by people who manage to remain unusually calm so that they are able to lie without their nervous systems reacting. Some people who come from countries where lying is endemic have the ability to lie while remaining physically calm. Is there anyone with this kind of background on your staff?"

Christopher looked pensive. "Everyone on the staff right now was born in America. They are all calm and unemotional in the office. I cannot tell if someone there is good at beating polygraph tests."

Mary said, "There is only one other possibility that I can think of. This might be an invisible man case, that is, a case where someone's presence on the scene of the crime was not noted. Has anyone left your employ recently?"

"Yes, the bookkeeper left about three weeks ago."

"Perhaps he left with some coins whose absence was not detected until a couple of weeks after he was no longer on the premises. Thus no one thought to subject him to a lie detector test."

"I never doubted Amin's honesty. Bookkeepers are noted for their integrity; their jobs depend on it."

"At this point he is the only one who was on the premises at the time of the theft who has not been tested."

"I will see what we can do about that," promised Christopher.

A few days later Claire telephoned Mary and exclaimed, "They caught him! You were right! It was the bookkeeper. When they notified him that he was to appear for a lie detector test, he tried to sell the eight escudos piece. The numismatist recognized the missing coin and notified the police. Amin was quickly apprehended and will remain in state custody for the foreseeable future."

"I wonder why he thought he could get away with it," Mary said.

"He was young and didn't realize how thorough security measures are in this business. And Mary, Christopher says to tell you that your presence is requested at our annual awards banquet in May. I have the feeling they will be giving you some kind of a reward for having solved the crime."

And so on a certain May evening Mary Stadeck was in attendance at the Hadley, Ryland & Martin awards banquet at the *Laurent* restaurant in mid-Manhattan On that gala occasion she was honored with the presentation of a gold sovereign depicting the youthful Queen Victoria as a Grecian maiden, which Christopher Martin said represented the firm's recognition of the recipient's youth and beauty and intellectual contribution.

The Baltic Memorandum

One sultry August evening I was visiting a friend, William Tremblay, in his apartment on Waverly Place near Washington Square in Greenwich Village. We were relaxing in his study, a room lined with bookshelves sporting titles such as *Primates in the Jungles of French Guiana* and *Scuba Diving for Atlantis*. I doubted that Tremblay had actually read the most eccentric of these works as he never alluded to them. I sometimes surmised that they had been left in the apartment by the previous owner. Then again, it may have been that he had picked them up in some secondhand bookstore in the Village and had simply never gotten around to reading them.

From his conversation one could tell that Tremblay had a classical bent. What he loved to talk about – and this topic was broad enough to span a number of divisions of intellectual inquiry – was human psychology. Here he waxed eloquent and occasionally profound. He liked in particular to discourse on the foibles of man, his character, his loves and his hates. Tremblay was not narrowly selective in his choice of analysts of the human condition but had evolved an eclectic approach to this study which allowed him to discuss Plato, William James and Sigmund Freud in the same sitting.

On this particular evening Tremblay was holding forth on the merits of the latest theatrical production at the Vivian Beaumont Theater when the bell rang. It was one Michael Muddle whom Tremblay promptly buzzed in. Our visitor was a slightly built man in a conventional gray suit. Tremblay introduced him to me as a private detective with whom he had worked on several matters. Muddle had an agitated air about him. His face perpetually wore a quizzical expression. His sentences had a tendency to end inconclusively, every segment being posed with an interrogative lilt at the end. He looked around the room as if hunting for something. At length he paused in his silent investigation and addressed Tremblay.

"I have had occasion to consult you before, and I was most grateful for your help last month in the Chatham ruby case and can never forget how you pointed out the clue of the scrambling lizard in the Cambridge folio incident. I trust you will be able to come to my aid again in what has turned out to be a most peculiar case."

"So what is the matter?" my friend asked.

Muddle looked doubtfully at me.

"You may rely on Philip. He is a trusted friend and will regard whatever is said here as confidential," Tremblay assured him.

Muddle then proceeded to tell us the following story.

"My client is a diplomatic representative of Estonia and occupies the position of First Secretary in their mission to the United Nations. As First Secretary, he has access to secret documents and possesses a top-level security clearance. Yesterday evening he took a sheaf of correspondence and other reading material home from the office. As his wife was out with friends, he dined alone and then sat down at his desk in the living room to read through his correspondence. He had scarce begun when he noticed that a top secret memorandum had inadvertently been included in the sheaf he had brought home. It was a memorandum from the Foreign Minister of his country to the Prime Minister and concerned sensitive negotiations they were currently undertaking with a superpower. Ordinarily one is not allowed to take such a document off the premises of the mission. Just as he was looking at it, the bell rang and the doorman announced that a Mr. Claude Morrow was in the lobby. My client had met Mr. Morrow in the course of his work on the boards of various civic institutions. He placed his briefcase on top of the papers on his desk and went to open the door for his visitor."

"Claude Morrow?" I interpolated. "I have played tennis with him at the Athletic Club."

Mr. Muddle nodded and continued. "My client noticed when he saw Mr. Morrow that he was dressed to the nines although he was visiting after business hours and might easily have changed to more casual attire. After preliminary inquiries after my client's family, Mr. Morrow began to discuss some issues facing the Metropolitan Opera on whose board they both sat. My client rose to pour a couple of drinks in the kitchen, leaving Mr. Morrow alone in the living room for perhaps all of three minutes. When he returned, his guest was reading the most recent issue of *The New Yorker*. At length he took his leave, and my client returned to his desk. It was at this time that he discovered to his consternation that the memorandum was missing. My client has no doubt but that Mr. Morrow took it while he was out of the room. What is more, Mr. Morrow has since contacted him to arrange for a dinner appointment. Naturally, my client has accepted, and they are to meet tomorrow evening."

"You said that there was something most peculiar about this case," Tremblay said, "but so far it seems very straightforward to me."

"I was about to come to that," Muddle continued. "My client lost no time in contacting me and asked that I obtain access to Mr. Morrow's apartment and conduct a search for the document there. Mr. Morrow's family has gone to the country and so he is currently living alone. Under these circumstances I had little difficulty in insinuating my way into his apartment while he was out and searching it."

"Without a warrant? You could be arrested, my good man," remarked Tremblay in mock surprise.

"I've done it before and I'll do it again," said Muddle. "It's a risk you have to take in this profession."

He paused and looked around the room again. Returning to his subject, he said, "Although I searched high and low – in the cabinets, the desk, the tables, sofa, chairs, behind paintings and under rugs – I was unable to find it."

"Did you get a good description of it?"

"Yes. It is a five-page memorandum from the Foreign Minister to the Prime Minister on a delicate international matter. It would be rather difficult to hide in a small area. I looked all over his apartment for a secret drawer or a wall safe but was unable to locate one."

"Is it possible that the man is carrying it with him or has taken it to his place of business?"

"Mr. Morrow is semi-retired from the financial industry and uses his residence as his office. Therefore, it is unlikely that he would have hidden the memorandum elsewhere. What is baffling to me is how a five-page document could disappear so completely. I have used the finest methods known to the science of detection and have come up with nothing."

"Perhaps he hid it on a microdot, in which case you will never find it," my friend said.

Muddle looked nonplussed.

Tremblay laughed and said, "Relax. I do not think he is so sophisticated. High technology may be used in international espionage, but what we have here is opportunistic low-tech thievery. In fact, I would argue that we are dealing with an ordinary kleptomaniac."

Muddle shrugged his shoulders.

Tremblay continued, "Perhaps the document is hidden in an obvious place."

"Obvious? William, whatever this document may be, it certainly is not obvious. If it were obvious, I should have found it by now."

Muddle broke off, bemused by Tremblay's suggestion. Tremblay assured the detective that he would do everything in his power for him and would contact him immediately if there were a breakthrough in the case.

After Muddle had left, Tremblay meditated a while and I, too, respecting his cogitations, was silent. "An interesting case," he said at last, breaking the silence. "A highly sensitive memorandum is stolen, presumably by a man who can have no professional reason for wanting it, that is, I am assuming Morrow is not a spy. He picks up the attaché case and sees documents, the secret memorandum being on top. He takes just that one, perhaps recognizing its highly confidential nature, and secretes it on his person. When the First Secretary returns, he affects to be reading a magazine, carries on a casual conversation and eventually leaves the apartment with the document. He subsequently contacts the First Secretary and invites him to dinner, presumably to discuss on what terms he will restore the memorandum. I think this is a case of blackmail. Whether the man is a kleptomaniac and is simply enjoying another person's pain or genuinely needs the money he expects to extort is relevant to our inquiry, however, as the answer to this question may give us an idea as to how and where he concealed the document. A straightforward thief who is hoping for a financial reward might hide the document in a conventional place. A kleptomaniac, however, who is out for psychological thrills might show his contempt for his victim in the way he hides the document. He might do something with it that would not occur to an ordinary larcenist. This theft is a matter of no small importance to the First Secretary. If he pays Morrow's price, he can have his document back and no one will be the wiser. If he refuses, he may lose his position and face charges of spying. Treason in Estonia may carry the death penalty. Hardly much of a choice there for the First Secretary. Of course, it is always possible that Morrow actually is a spy, and then he will want to use the document to blackmail the First Secretary into divulging more secrets. However the case may be, it is a matter of great urgency for the First Secretary. It is eight o'clock. Perhaps we ought to pay a call on Mr. Morrow this evening. What do you say, Philip? He is an acquaintance of yours."

"Yes, as I said earlier, I see him from time to time at the Athletic Club. I'm all for it, but I don't know what a social visit will accomplish. I doubt Morrow will give us the document just for the asking."

"Perhaps we won't have to ask for it. Perhaps we can find it and spirit it away without his knowing."

So saying, Tremblay ushered me out of his apartment and down into the street. A short while later we were welcomed at the Sutton Place duplex of Claude Morrow, a man in his late fifties with a self-confident, prosperous air. He explained that his wife and children were spending the summer in the country and that he went out to join them only on weekends. He was therefore unhappily condemned to bachelor status on weekdays. I engaged him on a topic I knew was close to his heart while Tremblay nonchalantly looked around the room. When our host offered us drinks, Tremblay readily assented and even accompanied him to the kitchen to continue the conversation. After a few minutes they returned, laughing over some amusing anecdote recounted by Tremblay. We chatted again for a while when suddenly Tremblay, in an excess of conversational exuberance, knocked over his drink, spilling it on his pants. He repaired to the kitchen to wash out the stain, emerging a few minutes later somewhat the wetter for the experience. Shortly thereafter we bade our host goodnight. Once out on the sidewalk, Tremblay telephoned Muddle and told him to meet us at the Waverly Place apartment. When we arrived, Muddle was waiting for us by the door. His hair was disheveled, his tie loosened, and he was carrying his jacket slung over his shoulder.

"You look none the worse for the wear, Michael," said Tremblay with a touch of irony.

"These cases get to me. I keep trying to solve them every which way."

Tremblay solicitously escorted us up to his apartment where he made sure we were comfortably settled and then began to hold forth.

"The data often appear to be undifferentiated as to significance in these cases," he opened, "and therefore they pose a mystery. One has to have a commitment to the truth or one will never be a good detective. Many people lack this commitment, and they go through life being mistaken about nearly everything outside of their everyday life."

He looked at us as if to find some sort of assent to his words. I nodded. Then he continued. "Once a detective has a set of sound principles, the data he is looking at take on some shape, and the matter at hand becomes a good deal less mystifying. The principles, of course, have to be correct in themselves, and they have to be applicable to the particular situation. For instance, if we know that thieves entering affluent neighborhoods are apt to dress better and more carefully than the residents, then a well-dressed individual found doing something of a dubious nature in an affluent neighborhood would immediately be suspected of entertaining nefarious intentions with respect to local property. However, if one is not aware of the principle that thieves and hired assassins tend to dress in their Sunday best when they have evil purposes, it might take longer to identify suspicious behavior as just that. It is possible, of course, to develop such a principle from a number of observations of the data."

When Tremblay paused in this disquisition, I stole a glance at Muddle. His usual quizzical expression had deepened into a look of utter bafflement. He stared wide-eyed at Tremblay. His arms dangled helplessly over the sides of his chair. With a sympathetic smile Tremblay broke the silence.

"My dear fellow," he said, "in the case before us the thief had hidden the state paper in an inobvious place. That is to say, in order to be inobvious about it, he had hidden it in an obvious place. He had tacked it up right in front of our noses."

Tremblay pulled some papers out of a pocket inside his jacket. On each sheet was a child's finger painting in garish green, red, orange and blue. When he turned over the pages one by one we saw the memorandum for which we had been looking.

"Morrow had these finger paintings securely tacked to a bulletin board in the kitchen. When I saw the finger paintings, I noticed at once that each was held down by four tacks. One or two would have done the job nicely, but Morrow wanted to discourage anyone from looking on the other side. He knew his apartment might be searched, and therefore he took the precaution of daubing paint on the back of each page. I saw them when I went to the kitchen with Morrow to fix the drinks. What clinched it for me was that in one corner of each sheet the paper was slightly torn where the staple had been removed. After we returned to the living room, I made a show of getting excited about the conversation and tipped over my drink on my pants. In order to wash off the stain, I went into the kitchen where I quickly removed the pages of the memorandum from the bulletin board and secreted them in my pocket. And so you may return them to your client."

The detective came to life, joyfully accepted the artistically enhanced memorandum and fled with his treasure.

"Is Morrow a kleptomaniac, a spy, an extortionist or any combination of the above?" I queried.

"Well, if he were a spy, the memorandum would have been off the premises right away," replied Tremblay. "As it is, the memorandum was, shall we say, 'decorated.' To me, this is the work of a kleptomaniac rather than of someone in financial straits. By turning it into a child's finger painting, he displayed a certain contempt for the document which leads me to conclude that he is probably a sadist. His motivation was psychological rather than economic."

"Then why did he contact the First Secretary if money were not his object?"

"He may have wanted to see his dismay. Perhaps Morrow is a good old-fashioned sadist who wanted to see the First Secretary's pain up close rather than just imagine it."

"Do you think he planned to ask for money?"

"Perhaps he had a specific sum in mind or perhaps he wanted to see what the First Secretary would offer. We cannot know for sure what his strategy was, but he was probably not above accepting any financial arrangement the First Secretary might have offered."

"That leaves a bad taste in my mouth," I said.

"Then let me offer you some Chardonnay, my good fellow," said Tremblay, "and I will entertain you with some thoughts on primates in the jungles of French Guiana."

The Case of the Disappearing Library

There is hardly a more isolated area than the sunlit hills and hollows of the Blue Ridge Mountains surrounding Asheville, North Carolina. Dwellings are sparsely distributed in this idyllic setting, and a man calls neighbor a fellow who lives half a mile down the road. The people are not unfriendly but, resident in the mountains for generations, they have developed certain idiosyncrasies and unique reference points. Having grown accustomed to living in isolation, they frequently regard outsiders with distrust. When riled by intrusions from the outside world for tax or other purposes, they have proven quite resourceful in maintaining their peculiar lifestyle. They are not unlettered and frequently spend the long evenings at home narrating old adventures and indigenous legends or simply reading out loud to one another from a small cache of books full of adventure and inspiration.

It was to just such a milieu that the Downings had relocated from New York City. A young couple, they found the rural pace of life much to their way of thinking. Timothy Downing was an artist and fell easily into a pattern of painting in an outlying shed in the morning, taking long walks in the hills in the afternoon, and indulging his passion for reading and music in the evening hours. His wife Mary would hardly feel uncomfortable with such a lifestyle for she had grown up in a rural setting in a family with avid intellectual interests. She was presently teaching in a high school in Asheville, and what leisure she had, after preparing lessons and dinner, she spent in much the same fashion as did her husband.

The Downings enjoyed inviting friends who lived up North to spend their vacations with them so that what might have proved to be a somewhat isolated existence had become a pleasantly social one. And so it happened that one Sunday evening in October the Downings were immersed in conversation with their house guest, William Tremblay, a private detective in New York City. Tim and William had gone to college together, and the two men had many happy memories to share. They regaled Mary with stories of undergraduate pranks and professorial quirks. Old cronies were recalled with merriment.

"Professor Hawthorne used to say in English literature class," Tremblay then remarked in a more pensive vein, "that you could tell a man by what he read. If he read the classics, he was a man to be taken seriously. If he confined his reading to professional journals, light fiction or simply the daily newspaper, he was a man without great perspective and insight. I see it somewhat differently. Once we're done with school, we follow our interests in selecting our reading material. That is why, I suppose, I have always resisted the suggestions of others as to what books I should read. Some people read in a desultory fashion, here and there, without any particular purpose. I, on the other hand, tend to pursue a certain interest for a while, read all I can on the subject, and then go on to something else. In this way I have answered a few key questions for myself and have built up areas where I have a reasonable amount of expertise. Do you find yourself doing the same?"

"The ghost certainly does!" exclaimed Mary.

Tremblay turned a blank, uncomprehending stare in her direction.

"Queer things have been happening in this house," she said, "ever since we moved in six months ago." She paused reflectively. "The house had not been lived in for several years before we came. The previous owner, an elderly woman, had died intestate, and there was a protracted battle in court over who would inherit the property."

"What do you mean by 'queer things?'" Tremblay asked.

"Oh, a number of things," Mary continued. "After we had been here a month or so, we began to notice books in different places on the shelves in the den. Tim rarely touches my books, but when I went to look for my *Emily Dickinson Reader* one day, it was not in its usual place. A few days later I found it with my Jane Austen books. I thought no more about the matter, assuming that Tim had taken a sudden fancy to Emily Dickinson and then had forgotten where I kept my collection on her. When this pattern had been repeated several times, I mentioned it to him and found, to my surprise, that he had not been reading the works in question. Other things have been happening as well. As you know, I go to work around 7:00 a.m., and Tim retires to his studio at the other end of the property perhaps an hour later. We have been returning in the afternoon to find windows open that we are certain we locked in the morning before leaving. To make matters worse, this is an old house, and sometimes it creaks and groans. There have been times, particularly on windy days, when I have had to keep a strong grip on my nerves on account of all the strange noises I hear in the house."

Mary paused and her husband picked up the conversational thread. "While we don't believe in ghosts in general, we are willing to accept the ghost theory as a working hypothesis for what has been occurring in the house. When we asked our nearest neighbor, Sam Thornton, who lives several hundred yards down the road, if he had seen anyone around the house, he said no. We asked him about the previous owners, but the stories he told were conventional family history. Sam is not a reticent man. If he were aware of anything peculiar about the history of the house, he would surely have told us. We have begun to be most particular about locking the house up tight before we leave in the morning. All the windows are locked shut. The garage is detached from the house, and the outside cellar door is always locked. The chimneys are also securely closed. So you see, we are plainly baffled by what is going on. Do you have any ideas about all this?"

Tremblay shook his head in the negative. "What are the chances I will meet your ghost during my stay?" he asked.

"We think we are haunted about once a week," replied Tim.

"I was expecting to remain in the house alone tomorrow and get some reading done while you two went off to work. Perhaps I can play librarian."

At this point Mary commented on the coolness of the nights in October, and the conversation turned to other topics.

The following morning, after his hosts had left for work, Tremblay wandered into the den. He selected a light novel from the shelves, eased into an armchair and lay his revolver, its safety catch off, on the end table next to his chair. He had a clear view of the entrance to the room and commanded a view out the windows on the acreage in the rear of the house. To tell the truth, he was intrigued by the mystery delineated the previous night by the Downings and hoped to solve it.

    He did not have long to wait. He was halfway into the second chapter of the novel when a noise put him on the alert. It was indistinct, nearly indiscernible. It may have been only the creaking of the house. He listened carefully and thought he detected footsteps. Then a door opened. He laid the book noiselessly on the end table. He picked up his revolver and pointed it at the doorway. A wizened old man wearing spectacles and clad in a gray sweater and slacks walked casually into the room. On seeing the revolver aimed in his direction and Tremblay's stern gaze fixed on him, he froze, shock and dismay registered on his face. Then he bolted to the door leading to the cellar and plunged down the steps. Tremblay charged after him in hot pursuit. He heard a crash.

    When he arrived in the cellar, the electric light was burning, but nary a soul was in sight. Recalling that the outside cellar door was always locked, Tremblay started to check every shadowy corner and indentation and to look behind every large object in the cellar, in short, in every place where a man might conceivably be hiding. No one was there. Convinced that his search had been thorough, Tremblay turned his thoughts to another possibility. There must be a secret entrance into the cellar, he reasoned. He began tapping the walls to test their solidity. He was in the midst of this painstaking project when suddenly he noticed a square of metal set into a knot in a floorboard. He tugged at the metal piece and lifted a trapdoor, revealing an iron-runged ladder descending into the darkness. He had discovered the exit used by the intruder, but where did it lead? He went back upstairs to avail himself of a flashlight. Taking the precaution of leaving a note for the Downings, he then returned to the cellar and let himself down through the trapdoor, climbing down the ladder into a room. His flashlight revealed a couple of old chests and a passageway leading out of the room. As he hurried along the passageway, he tried to keep track of his direction but had to give it up as hopeless because of the twists and turns. The passage wound along for several hundred feet and then came out in another room, this one full of old casks. A ladder indicated the means of egress. Tremblay climbed it and, lifting a trapdoor, found himself in the middle of a forest. There was no one in sight, not even a building. He decided he must be in the woods that began two hundred feet behind the Downings' house. There was no path, and therefore no means of tracking the old man any further. Tremblay decided to call it a day and returned to the house via the underground passage.

That evening his hosts were excited to learn that Tremblay had actually seen the intruder and had discovered his means of entrance. The two men descended to the passage and walked through to its exit in the forest. They found that in the darkness they were able to discern a light that they assumed came from the house since there were no other dwellings nearby. The following morning they called on Sam Thornton and in the course of the conversation elicited the information that a retired history professor was living with his daughter about a mile away. Thornton also confirmed that bootlegging had been a popular activity in the vicinity of Asheville during the era of Prohibition.

As for the rest, the contents of the casks turned out to resemble a fine old wine. The chests in the underground room contained a collection of elegant silverware which was immediately bestowed on William Tremblay in gratitude for his assistance. The Downings decided to make the acquaintance of the old professor whose subsequent visits lightened many an evening that would otherwise have been spent in more solitary pursuits. On these occasions the Downings and their guest conversed on a variety of literary and philosophical topics, rounding the evening off with a glass of wine of uncertain vintage. And ever after that whenever the Downings entertained guests from up North, they would regale them with stories about the mysterious ghost haunting the hills and hollows surrounding Asheville.

The Escalon Inscriptions

The morning sun filtered through the leaves of a yew tree and played on my bed in the Hamlet Room at the Shakespeare Hotel in Stratford-on-Avon. The sunlight slowly shifted and reached my face. It stroked me until I drowsily opened my eyes and peered at the watch I had deposited on the night table the previous evening. It was eight o'clock in the morning, time to be stirring. Undoubtedly my companion on this vacation, William Tremblay, a private detective in New York City, was already waiting for me in the dining room.

With all due speed I found my way downstairs to the lobby. As I entered the dining room, I saw Tremblay, impeccably dressed in casual sightseeing attire and seated at a table perusing the morning paper. He greeted me and, after waiting for me to give my order to the waitress, proposed that our touring take a slightly unconventional direction.

"We have a few days of leisure before we have to make a theatre date in London, Philip, so why don't we indulge a notion I have had to delve into a bit of archeology? We have seen everything noteworthy in the vicinity of Stratford. Perhaps we can spend a day looking for a historical site dating back to the time of King Arthur. Does that appeal to you?"

"What do you have in mind?" I was cautious at that hour of the morning.

"You know the English countryside abounds in the remains of history. Every river, hilltop and village has a legend or historical fact associated with it. Most of what we have seen so far belongs to the last five centuries. I propose to go further back in time, to peer through the mists separating us from an earlier age, and to see the world as it was in the days of King Arthur, after the last Roman legion had left Britain and Camelot shone brightly in the land."

"What do you propose to do?"

"A year ago a professor at Oxford, one Thomas Neyland, published a monograph in *The Historical Review* on a find of some inscriptions in Latin dating back to the time of King Arthur. They were chiseled into stones in Exmoor National Park in Somerset. Unfortunately, the professor kept the exact location to himself. I thought, if you agree, that we might devote a day to looking for it."

Having nothing better in mind, I assented to his plan. A short while later, we had gathered our belongings, checked out of the Shakespeare Hotel, and taken the road to Somerset. On the way Tremblay filled me in on the details. He had had the foresight to write to the Countryside Commission requesting information as to the exact location of the inscriptions. The reply was not encouraging, the Countryside Commission attributing the carvings to quarrymen in the nineteenth century.

"And what," asked Tremblay rhetorically, "is the likelihood that Exmoor quarrymen would be conversant in the Latin language or be interested in writing about King Arthur in that tongue? That is a farfetched hypothesis indeed. I fear the Countryside Commission is out of sympathy with this shard of archeology. Any site relating to our immediate ancestors is developed energetically, with plaques, museums, tour guides, etc., but a site dating back to early medieval times does not interest them. You have to remember that this archeological find has turned up wholly unexpectedly. We have a bit more history than we had previously thought, but the Countryside Commission has decided we can very well get along without it and has therefore decided to ignore it. Truth is always stranger than fiction, they say. If this really is an archeological site dating from Arthurian times, people ought to find out about it. Between an obscurantist Oxford don and an obstructionist Countryside Commission, how will the general public ever come to know the truth?"

He paused as another idea occurred to him.

"The Countryside Commission writes that the site is located on the east side of Escalon Bay near the town of Dunster in Somerset. Perhaps a ranger can tell us exactly where to go. I wonder where the ranger station in Exmoor National Park is located."

"We can drive to the park and look around."

Our decision taken, we found ourselves a couple of hours later driving past Bridgwater, Watchet, Dunster and Minehead. Then we turned off onto a country road heading into the moor. Oaks, ashes and rowans wooded the valleys. Purple heather and yellow gorse hugged the banks of myriad streams. Bracken and whortleberries abounded on the moor. It was a wild and romantic scene, set off by the orderly fields of an occasional farm. We asked directions from some children playing by the roadside and ten minutes later swung into the parking lot of the Exmoor National Park Ranger Station. Tremblay lost no time in putting an inquiry to the ranger on duty. The man answered that he was aware of the article describing the inscriptions but that he had no idea of their location. He said that many people had made inquiries, but he had not been able to enlighten them. Tremblay produced the letter from the Countryside Commission, and the ranger read it carefully. He then explained that Exmoor National Park also administered some outlying forested areas, one of which fit the description given us, that is, it lay near Dunster on the coast and included a small body of water called Escalon Bay. He rummaged around on some shelves and at length produced a map of the trails in the forest near Dunster. Tremblay took out a sheet of paper and drew a careful replica of the ranger's map, complete with alternate trails. As we drove back to Dunster, he analyzed our findings.

"How could we know that the ranger would not be able to put us on the exact trail?" Tremblay fumed. "We just assumed that since the Countryside Commission knew the whereabouts of the stone inscriptions, the ranger in charge would also know. Do you see how endemic the obscurantism operating in this case is? The Countryside Commission knows, but it does not communicate this information to its man in the field. The professor knows, but he does not tell the general public. And so the world turns, never finding out the truth. Everything depends on individuals. If no one takes an interest in a particular question, the answer will never be found or broadcast. The general public will be the poorer for not knowing." Having vented his opinion, Tremblay laughed. "Whether we find the inscriptions or not, we will have an interesting time of it, no doubt," he said and for the rest of the trip back to Dunster, he amused me with anecdotes of his adventures in detective work.

In this agreeable fashion we drove through the town of Dunster and a little farther along the road discovered the entrance to the forest bordering on Escalon Bay.

To our surprise, we found that the path was apparently unfrequented. Everything seemed as if it had been enchanted a millennium and a half ago. No animals rustled in the underbrush and no birds soared overhead. Of human vestiges we saw only a few paint swatches marking the trail. We plunged into the forest. For a while the path paralleled some freshly laid train tracks. Then it slipped away from this sign of the Industrial Age and entered an area strewn with hefty rock formations, the remains of an ancient ice floe. Shortly thereafter we came across a giant rock formation singularly cut as if the basement of a building had been hollowed out of it.

"A bit of quarrymen's ruins, Philip," Tremblay said. "There probably isn't anything here, but I'll have a look just the same."

So saying he leapt to the top of the rocks and examined them for traces of writing. I tried to follow suit, but found that the street shoes I had purchased in London made clambering around on rock formations a slippery business. I resolved to stay on the path and was glad that Tremblay appeared to be in no need of assistance.

We continued along the trail, stopping at every stony outcropping. Occasionally we caught glimpses of Escalon Bay shimmering through the trees. While Tremblay was off investigating rocky ledges, two men in their thirties came hiking along an adjoining path. I called to them, but they were so engrossed in their conversation that it took several shouts before I succeeded in breaking through their concentration. I told them we were looking for some Latin inscriptions dating from the time of King Arthur.

"I have been hiking in this forest for years, and I have never seen any stones with writing on them," said one. Then he added, "You might try up by the cliffs near the head of the bay." I thanked him for this advice, and the hikers moved on. When I recounted this conversation to Tremblay, he opted for continuing his thankless task.

A few minutes later, while Tremblay was off investigating ledges, a middle-aged couple came walking down the trail. When I asked them if they knew of any inscriptions, the woman, who apparently did not relate to strangers, continued walking as if I had not spoken, but the man courteously paused to reply. Unfortunately, he did not have any information.

After some time we passed beyond the area of rock formations and found ourselves in a sunny wood. Tremblay was in a ruminating mood.

"Philip, obviously the local people are not aware of the inscriptions. Since we entered the forest, we have been investigating every stone we have seen and have found nothing. Perhaps our inductive approach to solving this mystery has been all wrong. Let's see if we can't use a little deductive reasoning here. We should try to figure out where human beings would most likely settle in the vicinity of Escalon Bay."

"So what do you conclude using the deductive method?"

"Only this. Man tends to settle near fresh-water sources, along brooks, streams, rivers and lakes. Escalon Bay, however, is a salt-water body so it is unlikely that human beings would depend on it as a source of water. They would have to boil the salt water before they used it. For this reason it is likely they would settle near a stream running into the bay. Now where do you think that would be located?

"At the head of the bay," I replied, "farthest from the sea."

"Just so. We must look for a stream at the head of the bay on the east side."

We had now walked a considerable distance from the rock formations. I was getting tired.

I relayed my fatigue to Tremblay and added, "Why don't we go back to the bay? I would like to see it up close. We have passed it by in all the excitement."

Tremblay graciously acceded to my request although he was eager to get on with the hunt for the inscriptions, and we retraced our steps. At length we took a side path in the direction of the bay and came out on a huge rock formation high above the bay. After admiring the view for a few minutes and ruminating about what the sunsets would be like from this point, we headed back to the main trail via another path. Suddenly a rock formation loomed before us full of Latin inscriptions.

"Eureka! We found it!" I exclaimed. We then set about discovering and photographing all the inscriptions mentioned by Thomas Neyland.

"And to think that we would never have found this if I had not acceded to your request to have a look at Escalon Bay! I had wanted to continue the search, but I also wanted to be kind to you," Tremblay remarked afterwards. Then he said something that surprised me. "I think I have figured out Professor Neyland's motive in suppressing the exact location of the inscriptions. We, too, will have to keep this find a secret. Otherwise scavengers will chip away at the inscriptions and take home the pieces." And so the discovery of the Escalon inscriptions by the general public remains for a more enlightened age.

Providence

An opinion column in *Corriere della Sera* that Monday morning grabbed Mario Vacari's attention as he lingered over breakfast and perused the paper. The columnist was informing the public that a recent study in Britain had concluded that one-third of the people on the planet would be happier if they did not marry. There is such a thing as a vocation for marriage, the study concluded, and if an individual does not have that predisposition, he will not find happiness with any marital partner. In fact, he would be happier if he abstained from sex altogether.

Mario Vacari shook his head. That was not his case. He had no doubts about the fact that he was destined for marriage. He had only to find the person Divine Providence intended for him. On this account he had run into some difficulty in that he could not tell who loved him and who was only pretending.

It was a morning in late autumn, and the leaves in the garden were turning shades of orange in the crisp air. Mario had no eye for their beauty. The article had stirred up a train of thought that abstracted him from the present moment and its distractions. He wondered whether the sublime event of falling in love would ever happen to him. Absent-mindedly he stirred the coffee in a creamy porcelain cup edged with a gold design. His mind was far from his surroundings at the moment, and he did not care. He wanted to linger on his thoughts.

Mario was seated at one end of a blond aspen table in the dining room of the contemporary home he had purchased on the outskirts of Rome. The downstairs boasted a white motif and parquet floors offset with pale blue area rugs. A few paintings of northern Italian scenes graced the walls. While assenting to the decorator's suggestions with respect to these public rooms, Mario had left the extra bedrooms upstairs unfurnished. His own bedroom was modestly furnished, awaiting the discretion of the bride he hoped one day to carry across the threshold. This morning he found himself preoccupied with this very question.

For a number of years he had had little idle time on his hands. He had grown up the scion of a family prominent in national affairs. His father had held a seat in the Chamber of Deputies for decades until one day he was involved in a car accident. Thereafter, it fell to Mario to uphold the family honor on the national scene. He had run for and won his father's seat in Parliament and had divided his time judiciously between Rome and his family home in Milan ever since.

Mario had been quite successful in pursuing his legislative agenda, but this had meant putting his personal life on hold. He had somehow managed to be so busy since he had stepped into his father's shoes that he had had no time to figure out much of a strategy for finding himself a wife. Not that it was difficult to attract women. No, that was not the problem at all. Women were constantly casting alluring smiles in his direction, hoping to attract his attention. They all wanted to be the wife of a Deputy. That was the problem. Mario despaired of finding someone who would love him for himself. All the young women he met were social climbers. He represented a position in society to them and was not really a person in his own right. Mario knew from observing society marriages that climbers were adept at pretending they loved a man until they had a marriage contract in hand, after which they might not bother about his feelings at all. Mario was wary of social climbers.

Picking up the porcelain coffee cup, Mario noticed that its contents had grown cold. His manservant Nicola appeared and cleared away the dishes. It was time to go to the office.

As he drove along, Mario continued to contemplate his personal life. His sister Daria had talked to him about falling in love. She said that when she first met her husband, it was love at first sight, i.e., they had a mystical experience, and afterwards they just knew they were meant to marry. Mario accepted this. His parents likewise had fallen in love suddenly. Mario thought that was the way it would be for him.

He was getting older, however. He was thirty at his last birthday, and there was no romance on the horizon. He had a recurring daydream that there was a beautiful young girl out there and he was waiting for her to grow up. One day he would meet her and they would fall in love. That was Mario's dream. He believed in it, but it had not yet materialized.

When he arrived at the Chamber of Deputies, he parked his car and emerged to begin his official day.

Around noon a thought came to him out of the blue. She does not love her family anymore. He had a sinking feeling in the pit of his stomach. He felt suddenly depressed. He got up to tell his secretary Miss Sanpietro that he would skip his customary working lunch with his staff and would dine alone on the Monday special.

He closed the office door and sat down again at his desk to think. He still had that depressed, sinking feeling. It was like a weight in his stomach pulling him down. His dream flashed before his eyes. He saw his beloved, but this time she was not happy. She was not even beautiful. She had lost her charm. She had lost her family love. Her family love was what Mario had been counting on. That was what he was looking for. He wanted someone who would love him. He did not want someone who had a terrific social personality but did not care about family. Mario was devastated. His world came tumbling down.

Miss Sanpietro, a trim, eldering woman he had inherited from his father, brought in his lunch. He thanked her and managed a shadow of a smile. He would have to eat or he would not be able to get through the next few hours.

He continued to feel miserable and finally pushed away the dessert. No sense enjoying anything when there was no love in his life.

For a couple of weeks Mario went through emotional devastation. He traveled abroad on a junket with other deputies from Lombardy. He was busier than ever upon his return. He attended some soirées for party members and a concert. He even went to a reception at the American embassy. His feeling of misery would not go away. His beloved did not love her family anymore. She had lost her inner happiness.

Sometimes the proverb "God never closes a door but He opens a window" floated into his mind. Only this thought kept him going.

Then one day around 11:30 a.m. a lovely young woman with dark blonde hair named Miss Elisabetta Intili walked into his life. She was representing a national pro-life organization and had come to his office to explain why he should favor pro-life legislation when it came up in the Chamber of Deputies. While Mario listened to her prepared remarks, an extraordinary sensation came over him. He thought the same phenomenon was happening to her. As he looked at her through a mystical haze, he saw that she was not only beautiful on the outside but also beautiful on the inside. Mario was mesmerized. They looked at each other in a somewhat helpless fashion. When she paused in her delivery, he encouraged her to continue. Then he gave himself up to the delight of looking at the vision before him. He easily came to the conclusion that he would like to see her again. At a break in her presentation he asked her to call him Mario and when she did, he slipped into calling her Elisabetta. He invited her to have lunch in his office while she continued to explain the pro-life position on various bills before the legislature. She agreed and they spent a very pleasant lunchtime together, the euphoria continuing unabated. Mario made sure he had her number so that she could return for further explanations. Then he let her go.

He did not let her go in his thoughts, however. She seemed to be the solution to all his dilemmas. He thought Elisabetta loved her family and would be able to love a husband and children. She was not a climber who would not care about him once she had a legal hold on his wallet.

He called her into his office again. The euphoria was still there. This time he tried to take their relationship to the next level.

"Elisabetta, a man in my position has hardly any private life. Everything I do is watched by the scandal sheets, ready to relay it to the voters at large. From the time I leave my home in the morning until I return at night I am onstage. Thus I have to be circumspect in all my dealings with people. I cannot say anything in a personal vein or it will become the next day's gossip."

She nodded sympathetically.

"Having said that, I am wondering if you would like to go to dinner tonight at a little restaurant I know that is a bit out of the way. The people there don't seem to know who I am, and I feel like I am just one of the folks."

Elisabetta laughed and nodded. "Yes, I would love to. I am a little curious as to where you might be unknown."

"*La Lanterna Cinese*," Mario grinned, "where the owner is not exactly a native-born Italian."

And so it was settled. Mario would pick her up that evening on a certain corner in Trastevere and they would drive together to the restaurant.

And in this fashion Mario Vacari's status as an eligible bachelor around town came to an abrupt end the following June, and his confidence that Divine Providence was indeed managing his affairs was restored.

A Fortune

As Anthony Donner stepped out of a midtown lobby onto fashionable Park Avenue, a swirling snowstorm enveloped him. White flakes caught at his hair, changing him from a youth into Father Time in the course of a few seconds. Frosty pellets blown by the December wind assaulted his face until his cheeks were rosy from their sting. The combination of snow-dusted hair and pink cheeks transmuted Anthony's Father Time into a merrier figure, perhaps a Santa Claus if he had been dressed for it.

But no one looking into Anthony Donner's eyes would have mistaken him for Santa Claus. His eyes were far from merry. Where laughter, surprise, benevolence and warmth were wont to gleam hung a dull curtain of despair. Anthony, with a Master's degree in Communications and Technology, had spent the day seeking employment, and the day was coming to an end without his having found any. This had been the case for a couple of months filled with peregrinating all over Manhattan filling out endless questionnaires, taking tests and interviewing – in short, enduring every indignity that could possibly be visited on a man who is looking for work without his being in the least bit able to lodge a protest or get up a petition. He was only the fiftieth candidate Personnel had run through its maze in the obscure hope of sorting out an agreeable person with intelligence and experience who was willing to work for a modicum of pay in the last subdivision in a department so far down the corporate ladder that it was off the organizational chart altogether. For this obscure position Anthony had no doubt that Personnel would deem him overqualified, and hence in his better moments he hovered between a form of gallows humor and dark despair.

    The white crystals gusting around him contrasted so sharply with his black thoughts that he looked up with a vague sense of having been interrupted. Then he saw a lad of thirteen distributing a free newspaper. Bracing himself against the snowy bombardment, the boy managed to advertise his product to all who would listen within a radius of five feet. Mindful of the "Help Wanted" section, Anthony took a copy.

    "Have a good day, sir," the lad said.

    Anthony plunged back into the obscurity of the storm. His face downward as he picked his way through the snowy drifts, he almost missed her. As it was, he with his head down and blinded by the driving snow and she carrying shopping bags and in the same bent posture almost missed each other. They did not miss each other, however, but collided, the effects of such collision buffered by her packages, her fur coat and the snowdrift upon which she immediately sat down. Anthony, better able to withstand collisions due to his bulk, was left standing and was beside the young woman in a thrice.

    "I'm terribly sorry, ma'am," he said, bending over the pert, young face looking up at him with more amusement than shock. "Are you all right?"

    "I'm perfectly fine," the vision replied. He helped her to her feet and watched while she dusted the snow off her coat. She added, "This is a confetti wonderland. I am surprised there are not more collisions."

"Yes, on a day like today it is better if one doesn't have to go out at all," he smiled. After restoring her shopping bags to her, Anthony bade her farewell and watched her disappear into the storm. When he came back to himself, he espied a small package in the snow. The young lady had dropped it. Scooping it up, he rushed after her, but she had disappeared into the holiday crowd. Reluctantly, he abandoned the effort and directed his steps to the *Savoy*, a coffee shop on Madison Avenue where he often rendezvoused with his friends.

It occurred to him that the package might contain a clue as to the identity of the owner. So thinking, he entered the *Savoy* and sat down at a table in the corner. He ordered a cup of coffee and then proceeded to undo the bundle. To his utter astonishment, he found a diamond necklace, earrings and a bracelet in it. While he was contemplating this unexpected trove, a group of young people burst into the coffee shop joking and laughing and propelling each other into the center of the dining area. One of them, Brett Hudson, saw Anthony and directed the others to his table. They set about rearranging the furniture and making themselves comfortable around the newly elongated table. When everyone had settled down, Brett remarked on the contents of Anthony's package. "Where did you get the diamonds?" he asked. No sense in not getting down to brass tacks right away. Sue Ellen Koeffler tried the bracelet on.

"I found them," responded Anthony, nervously watching the bracelet.

"You found them! Congratulations!" exclaimed Brett. "What a fantastic piece of luck! Where did you find them? Maybe I can find some too." The others expressed a similar interest. Sue Ellen picked up the necklace and endeavored to put it on.

"In a snowdrift on Park Avenue, but this was the only package I saw." Anthony was by now trying to retrieve the necklace from Sue Ellen. She handed it over reluctantly.

"It's just a package I found in the snow. I have no idea of the owner's name. I'll just have to hand it in to the police." While he was saying this, Anthony held out his hand. Sue Ellen slowly took off the bracelet, kissed it and dropped it into his open palm. Anthony started to wrap the parcel up again, to the immense chagrin of Brett and his companions who had been feasting their eyes on it.

"Finders keepers, Anthony," said Brett. "You don't have to give it to the police. Think of all the nice things you could do with the money. You could take us all out to dinner, and at a fancier restaurant than the *Savoy*. You could take a trip to Europe. Who knows what opportunities might develop. You can always use a little extra cash. If you can't think of anything to do with it, give it to me. I'll think of something."

All his friends concurred. By this time Anthony had succeeded in retying the package and was signaling the waitress for his check.

"Finders keepers, Anthony," Brett reiterated. "It's okay to keep something you find, especially when you don't know who lost it."

Anthony smiled and continued his preparations for departure.

"Finders keepers, losers weepers, Anthony. Think about it. You could use the money," Brett urged again, and all his friends echoed his sentiments.

At length Anthony paid his bill and found his way out of the coffee shop. Back on the sidewalk, he mulled over Brett's words. It was true. He could use the money in his reduced circumstances. He could sell the jewelry in such a way that no one would be able to trace it to him. The commandment "Thou shalt not steal" quietly occurred to him. He remembered Miss Edelstein's religion class in which she had told him and his fellow students that the Golden Rule, "Do unto others what you would have others do unto you," indicated indirect reciprocity. Miss Edelstein explained that "others" was indeterminate. That means that whatever we do unto A, B will do unto us. Maybe A is a little brother and cannot directly pay us back, but someone else will. Anthony started having visions of his possessions disappearing if he failed to return the lost diamonds. He quickly found a police station and rid himself of the package.

The next day his mother took a message over the telephone from a certain Catherine Prince who wished to thank him personally for returning her jewelry. Would he please call on her at home? It was an address on Fifth Avenue. When Anthony repaired there on the following day, his fortunes began a steady upward climb.

[handwritten correction: Kathryn Price]

Made in the USA
Charleston, SC
08 February 2012